The C'est La Vie Guarantee

EMILY CRUZ

THE C'EST LA VIE GUARANTEE

To the friends who have shaped me, supported me, and loved me.

THE C'EST LA VIE GUARANTEE

CHAPTER 1: KAIA

"We regret to inform you we will be letting you go from the firm. Please collect your belongings from your office, and security will escort you to your car."

He said all of this without looking up.

"You're firing me?" I ask, not sure I fully understood him.

My hands grip the armrests of the overpriced and incredibly uncomfortable chair I'm sitting in. At least I was sitting when he told me. I look up at Martin, the department's managing partner, also known as the man who just tilted my entire world on its axis. He's sitting at his fancy desk that overlooks the Space Needle, completely unbothered that he's just told me I'm being fired from the company I've put my literal blood, sweat, and tears into for the past six years. *Six. Years.* He's taken one minute out of his day to throw the biggest possible wrench into my ten-year plan, and will probably head out right after this conversation to an overpriced dinner that he'll bill to a client and never think about it again.

"I don't understand. We had a department-wide meeting two days ago and there was no mention of layoffs or anything."

In fact, two days ago, I had been assigned a rather large and tedious project, and I distinctly remember him trying to lighten the load by telling me what an asset I was to the team, and that they were lucky to have me on board.

"Kayla, I'm sorry to have to do this." Oh, that's wonderful. He doesn't even know who I am. I'm not sure if that makes me feel better or worse.

"It's all got to do with seniority, billable hours, and client retention—it's out of my hands. But you're a smart girl, you'll find somewhere else to work. We're happy to provide a reference if needed."

"It's Kaia." That's all I can manage to say. I don't say anything about the insane amount of hours I've worked the past six years, or the fact that my entire life practically revolves around this firm.

"Right, right! Kaia, I'm so sorry. I would love to stay and chat, but I have a meeting in five minutes. Make sure you set up your exit interview with HR before you leave the building today, and give them your personal email. Your email for the firm won't be active after today."

"Sure thing," I say through gritted teeth, fighting back tears.

"Oh, and don't forget to turn in your key card on the way out, Maya. We have highly sensitive documentation in this office, and we wouldn't want a breach of security," he says while looking at his computer.

"Kaia. It's still Kaia." I say, my voice strained and clipped.

Do not flip him off, I think. Be the bigger person, Kaia.

"Right, yes! Kaia. My apologies. Security will see out." He waves his hand, gesturing for me to shut the door as I'm leaving. I shut it very nicely and quietly, instead of slamming it shut like I want to.

Proud of myself for not saying something I'd later regret, I hastily make my way to the bathroom. I let the door close quickly behind me and place my hands on either side of the sink, looking down at my shoes.

My tan loafers are spotted with wet marks, and I realize that I've started crying.

Why am I even crying? I think to myself. *I hated this job.*

It was hard not to when my boss was a complete jerk.

For legal purposes, we'll call him Kurt.

Kurt is truly the bane of my existence and the main reason I have workplace anxiety. He is exactly what you picture when you think of a young partner at an uber-successful law firm: tall, full of himself in his perfectly-pressed designer suits, always has a soy latte in hand and condescension on his face.

When I first started working for Hadley & Scott, an up-and-coming corporate law firm, he was on track to become partner, so he was *almost* enjoyable to work with while he ran the race and schmoozed the higher-ups. I wouldn't say he was kind, exactly, but he was…kind-adjacent.

That kindness became nonexistent last year when he was promoted. Between his rising star status and his high-profile cases, Kurt is now one of the most powerful partners at the firm, and he likes to make sure that's known through demeaning remarks and near impossible-to-meet standards.

I spend every waking minute at work trying to ensure the happiness of a man who is continuously disrespectful to those around him. Meanwhile, *he* spends every waking minute at work ensuring I know my work isn't up to par, I've missed something, or that someone else could do my job better.

But that was before…when I *had* a job. A well-paying job. A job that had me on track to make partner.

I wipe my face and stare at my reflection in the mirror. Black mascara is streaked across my face, and my cheeks are flush with embarrassment and anger. I feel unseen and under appreciated, despite my ridiculous dedication to this job.

I started working here because I wanted to make a difference in the lives of others, and I felt like I did that at the beginning. The lines got blurred somewhere along the way, and the work I was doing became less and less meaningful. For a long time now, I've felt like the human junk drawer of the office—taking on all the work that no one else wanted to do, but I did it anyway because I wanted to be helpful.

I focus on my reflection again. Beyond the ruined makeup and teary eyes, I don't recognize the girl staring back. Once, I was fresh out of law school with a sparkle in my eye and hope in my smile. Now, all I see is a lack of fulfillment written all over, especially in the way my mouth tilts down—the lack of smile lines present when joy marks your life.

What's happened to me? More so, how did I let this happen?

I feel like a shell of myself, like I've forgotten my dreams and why I wanted to be a lawyer. Not to mention, I've forgotten anything sort of resembling self-care.

I miss the girl who started at this firm, bright-eyed and ready to take on the world. The one who'd do whatever it took to pursue what was right and just. I miss her. She was feisty but empathetic. Determined, but flexible.

The girl looking back at me in the mirror looks sad and hardened by life. She looks closed off to new opportunities and risk-taking. She looks tired and uncertain about what comes next.

I rinse my face and swallow back fresh tears, not

about the job I just lost, but the version of myself I lost along the way.

I shuffle my feet to my desk, still processing what happened.

I just got fired.

I'm unemployed.

Jobless.

I have no stable income.

The thoughts stack up like a multi-car pileup in my brain.

An empty box is waiting for me on my desk; someone must've put it there while I was having a moment in the bathroom. I think back to the conversation that has completely changed the trajectory of my life, a conversation I will replay in my head over and over again and ruminate on all the arguments I could have delivered with ease if I could only go back in time.

At least he waited until the very end of the day to call me into his office, undoubtedly to avoid a scene afterward, because pretty much everyone has gone home.

"Bad day?"

The voice startles me, and I turn to find arguably

my favorite person at this law firm, Layla.

Layla's been here for about ten years. She's a partner in a separate department, and while she might not know it, she's been my secret mentor ever since I started here. If she was the partner I worked with primarily, my experience at this job would be vastly different, in a good way—In the *best* way.

But unfortunately, I rarely worked with Layla.

"*Bad* doesn't even begin to cover it," I say. "I just got fired."

Layla gasps. "You did not. Why?"

"I have no idea," I say honestly. "Martin's explanation was almost nonexistent."

Layla comes around my desk and wraps me in a hug. Though this is shaping up to be the worst day of my life, her presence here is already lifting my spirits.

I know everyone has a lot on their plate here, and I also know that a lot of people at this firm put the same "I want to help people" line in their law school application essays, but somewhere along the way, the stress, money, and power changes people.

But not Layla.

Truly, she is one of the nicest and most compassionate people I've ever met, which is why I think so highly of her. She and her husband are both lawyers and, in addition to their corporate jobs, they offer pro bono services to those who need legal counsel but can't afford it. Her workload has got to be at least double those of the managing partners who yell at staff members for every mistake, and yet, she extends the same kindness to everyone, no matter what.

Simply put, all hail Queen Layla. Layla for President.

We hit it off immediately when we met, and she's been my office fairy godmother ever since.

Three years ago, I was assigned to a case that Layla had taken on. I didn't know her at the time, but I knew *of* her. Her reputation as a managing partner who was an absolute delight to work with preceded her. Basically, she was the attorney version of a unicorn. I was so used to Kurt and his management style that I would've been happy working with someone who came off as mildly rude, maybe even someone who didn't really talk to me much at all. All I wanted was to do my job well and get on with my life. So, you can imagine my surprise once I met Layla and had a front-row seat to how she works.

We were nearing the end of the case we were working on, and honestly, we weren't sure if we were going to win. There was a suspicion that opposing counsel was doing some shady stuff with their witnesses, and we decided we needed to put in some late hours to gather our evidence for court the following day.

Usually, working late is the bane of my existence, but for Layla? You could find me at the office at eleven p.m., energy drink in hand and a big smile on my face.

In fact, *because she's Layla*, all night she tried to convince me to go home. Every half hour. She told me that she had it handled and that I needed to rest for court in the morning. But we weren't even halfway through evidence, and she and I both knew that she didn't have time to go through everything on her own. She's *incredible* at her job, but she's not actually a superhero—at least not that I can prove.

I convinced her that I wasn't going anywhere until we were done, so we ordered takeout from a nearby diner that stayed open late. We sat on the floor, eating and chatting between bouts of silence while we flipped through the remainder of evidence for our case.

I remember I didn't get home until two a.m., and it felt absolutely inhumane when my alarm went off at six the next morning.

My checklist for getting ready that morning was minimal:

A nice court-approved outfit that isn't pajamas? *Check.*

Brush the blueberry pancake flavor off of my teeth? *Check.*

Comb through my hair so I don't look like the girl from *The Ring*? *Check*, *check*, and *check*.

I got to the courthouse with a few minutes to spare but didn't have time to grab myself a coffee, so you can imagine my surprise and relief when Layla entered the foyer, two coffees in hand, one extended in my direction.

"Is this for me?" I asked, shocked, gratitude dripping from every word.

"Of course! If you're feeling anything like I am after last night, you're gonna need it."

I reached out and grabbed it with both hands, closing my eyes and savoring every drop of that first sip.

I opened my eyes to see Layla looking at me, amused.

"Sorry," I laughed. "I just really needed this. Thank you."

She smiled. "Anytime, Kaia. Thanks for helping on this case. Because of you, I think we have a good shot at winning."

Because of me? Pride swelled within me at her words of appreciation. I wasn't used to that at this job.

She leaned over and whispered in my direction, "Also, your shirt is inside out."

Of course it was. I looked down and confirmed that the giant seams on my yellow chiffon blouse were on full display.

My cheeks flushed, but I gave her a small smile, feeling only mildly embarrassed. "Whoops. Thank you."

In my defense, I had gotten ready in the dark... with my eyes closed.

"I've got your back, Kaia," she said with a soft confident smile.

And she meant it. Ever since then, she's been looking out for me. I absolutely would not have made it the last three years at this firm without her.

"So," Layla starts when she pulls free of the hug, "When is your trip?"

I look at her like I have no idea what she is talking about because *I have no idea what she is talking about.*

"When your friend stopped by to drop off a coffee to you the other day, I heard her mention a really fun girl's trip," she explains. "And…not to be insensitive here, but you have some extra free time on the horizon. Now is kind of the perfect time to go and get a much needed break."

"Yeah…" I start. "My best friends have this idea that we should take a girl's trip to Paris, but I'm not entirely sold on it."

"Look, I'm not trying to push you, but since we are office besties, I feel like I have to tell you: take the trip. You have the rest of your life to accomplish whatever it is you were hoping to accomplish here. You won't always be young and able to explore the world with your best friends. And, for what it's worth, I think you need to go." She looks at me, empathy and understanding radiating off of her. "Not *should* go, Kaia. *Need.* It's okay if that's not practical in the traditional sense. It doesn't have to be practical to be worth it."

How do you argue with that

You don't, I remind myself. Layla's a better lawyer than you.

Maybe it'd be wise to take her advice then. I give her a small smile and nod, taking her words to heart.

Once she's gone, I pack up the contents of the office, where I've spent more time the past six years than I did anywhere else. I take my framed degrees off the wall and place them in the box first, along with some reference books from law school that I'd used more times than I could count since starting here.

I unpin Polaroid pictures of me, Adelina, Callie, and Havannah and tuck them away in the corner of the box. When I was having a tough day at work, these pictures served as a reminder of what a great support system I have, and it helped motivate me to put my head down and get the job done.

I take down the first email I ever received from a client after working with them on their case. The email was a simple thank you note, letting me know how much they appreciated my help and what an impact it had on their family. I printed it out as soon as I received it and taped it up in my cubicle, because it reminded me why I got into this line of work, and why I needed to continue—to help those who needed it most. Every time I was assigned a project no one else wanted, or got yelled at by a partner, I read this email and told myself that if I stuck it out, I'd eventually get back to that kind of work.

I finish packing my things—stuffing six years into one box—and turn around to see one of the security guards, Saul, who has been here for twenty years and is one of the nicest men you'll ever meet. I call him Saul Blart, Law Cop, and he thinks it's the funniest thing he's ever heard. I'm gonna miss him and his dad jokes.

His empathetic eyes meet mine. "I'm sorry, Kaia. I hate to see you go."

"Me too," is all I can manage to say.

He escorts me to the third floor of the parking garage and waves as I walk to my car. "Take care of yourself, Kaia. You're gonna do big things in life, I just know it!"

"Thanks, Saul. I appreciate that," I say with a quick wave as I get in my car.

"I'm gonna do big things…like lay in bed, eat ice cream, and watch *Legally Blonde* on repeat for the next three weeks," I whisper to myself sarcastically.

As I drive through the winding parking garage and onto the street, the dread sets in.

What the hell am I going to do now? The thought quickly pops into my head, and right when I am about to spiral into a panic, I know exactly what I need to do.

Call my mom.

CHAPTER 2: KAIA

I call her as soon as I get home. And because it's impossible to hold anything in at the sound of your mom's soothing voice, I break down immediately, mumbling, "I got fired," in between sobs and blowing my nose.

"Oh, sweetie! I'm sorry," my mom attempts to console me.

"Do you want us to come over?" my dad asks, and I know I've been put on speaker.

"I can bring dinner. And some cookies," my mom offers.

A laugh escapes me mid-sob, and I tell her that they don't need to make the drive, though I appreciate the offer. My moms homemade oatmeal chocolate chip cookies are the best.

Once I compose myself, my parents express how happy they are that I no longer work for Hadley & Scott. They hated how I was treated there, and say they "can't wait for me to find my dream job!"

Me too.

"So, Kaia-bug, what do you think you'll do next job-wise? No rush, of course! You take as long as you need to find something you love," my mom says.

"I don't think I'll start looking for new jobs right away. I'm gonna try to do this new thing called resting. I hear it's all the rage these days."

Humor is my way of pretending I'm not struggling as much as I am. Humor is comfortable, so I cling to it for dear life.

"Well, good. I'm glad to hear you're planning to finally get some rest, sweetheart." My mom's voice is such a comfort, her love palpable even through the phone.

"How are the girls?" My mom asks about them every time we talk. "When's the next girl's night? I love that you guys do that!"

"The girls are doing great. They keep talking about this trip to Paris they want to go on," I say. "And I'm not sure when our next girl's night is, though it doesn't matter since my schedule is now *wide* open."

My mom gasps, followed by something that sounds like silverware falling onto the floor. "Oh my gosh! A trip to Paris! Kaia, that sounds like so much fun. And what perfect timing! You've always wanted to go, I'm so excited for you."

"Woah, woah, woah, Mom," I laugh. "I'm not going. I told them they should go anyway, though."

Silence.

"Mom, you there?"

When she chimes in again, her voice has gone up a few octaves, like it does when she's anxious or really fired up about something. "What do you mean, you're not going? Were you not invited?"

"Of course I was. It was actually sort of my idea. I just don't think it's the best idea right now. I need to find a job, not prance around the streets of France, pretending like my problems don't exist and I don't have bills to pay."

I hear some rustling, like my mom is digging through her purse or something.

"Oh, honey. Those are all valid concerns, and I appreciate how responsible you are, but this might be exactly what you need."

Why does everyone keep saying that?

"What I need is a stable job," I counter, my tone more frustrated than I intend.

My mom whispers something to my dad, and he whispers something back, too quiet for me to make out what they're saying.

"What is happening?" I ask.

"Let us pay for your trip!" my mom practically shouts.

Her enthusiasm is so sweet, but she just doesn't get it.

"What? No. No way," I say adamantly.

"Kaia, sweetie, I want you to have this experience. If you don't want to go to Paris, fine, but pick somewhere else and we'll pay for it! Our treat, no strings attached."

"Look, I appreciate the offer. It's incredibly sweet of you guys, but—"

My mom cuts me off.

"Kaia Joelle, you've been working hard for *years* without a significant break. You always do the right thing, the practical thing, and I admire that about you."

Whenever my mom uses my middle name, I know she means business.

My dad tries to cut in.

"Wait your turn, Kevin. Honestly, Kaia, your work ethic and dedication to helping others is something I am ardently proud of, but while you're taking care of others…you need to consider taking care of yourself, too. Rest is so crucial to ensuring that you can show up as your best self in your daily responsibilities."

I sigh. I hate when she's right.

I stare blankly at the wall across from my couch and realize with my parents offering to pay for my trip —which I would still never let them do—I'm fresh out of arguments, especially in response to the TED Talk my mom just delivered.

"So, does that mean you'll think about it?" she asks, excitement already building—I can almost see the excited look on her face through the phone.

My dad is quietly chanting, "Yes! Yes! Yes!" in the background, and I imagine him raising his arms in the air triumphantly with every word.

"I will *think* about it…but don't get your hopes up, okay, Mom? I'm still not convinced this is the right time for a trip like this."

The frantic knock at my door lets me know that the first of my rescue squad has arrived. Before I left work earlier, I texted my three best friends from the car. All I said was, SOS. Anyone free to meet me at my place at 9?

Each of them responded with some form of yes, and Havannah said she'd bring wine.

My comfort drink of choice tonight was a close tie between an ice-cold Sprite and Dr. Pepper, but ultimately Dr. Pepper won. Although, I may need a glass of wine after I have to relive the day I've just had.

I open the door to Havannah, an empathetic smile on her face, a bottle of red wine in one hand and a bag of Goldfish in the other.

Oh, she brought the big guns tonight.

I waited to dive into my disaster of a day until Lina and Callie showed up, which luckily was within ten minutes of Havannah's arrival. We settle in on the couch, cuddled under an array of cozy blankets with an assortment of snacks and drinks before us, completely prepared for the evening.

"So, what's up, Kai?" Adelina asks.

"Yeah, how can we help?" Callie asks.

"We've got your back," Havannah says, putting her arm around my shoulders. "Unless you killed someone. Even with your lawyer skills, I don't think we can defend that."

"You didn't kill someone, did you?" Lina asks.

I shake my head and take a deep breath, followed by a long sigh.

"I got fired today."

"WHAT?" Adelina shoots up from where she's sitting, spilling a bit of her drink on Callie.

"Woah, woah, woah! Slow down there, hot shot."

"Sorry," Adelina says absentmindedly, gaze locked on me. She sits back down and wipes Callie's arm off with the sleeve of her shirt.

"*You* got fired? You're one of the best things that have ever happened to that firm. What the hell do they think they're going to do without you?" Adelina says with conviction.

"That's sweet, Lina, but they were fine before me, and they'll be fine without me. They've got a lot of great employees."

"Yeah, and you were one of the best ones."

Adelina will hammer home her point until I concede.

"Okay, maybe I was…but now I'm not, and I've decided that's okay," I say, unsure if I'm trying to convince myself or them.

"I'm sorry, Kai," Callie says and reaches over to hug me.

Havannah and Adelina follow suit, promptly signaling the waterworks from me.

"I promised myself I would *not* cry tonight," I say through a half-laugh, half sob.

"Let it out, girl. We've got plenty of wine and snacks for this," Havannah says and hands me a tissue.

"Thank you. Seriously, you guys are the best friends I could ever ask for and I appreciate you responding so enthusiastically to my very dramatic SOS."

"Of course, we love you! We're here, *always*," Havannah says.

"What she said," Adelina adds with a smile.

"Yeah, what they said," Callie chimes in.

And it's true. They've always been here for me, and me for them. And while a lot of things about my life may change, showing up for one another won't.

A few hours later, I'm in the kitchen, rinsing some dishes in the sink when the girls make their way in from the living room. They crowd around the island, giving me a collective mischievous and somewhat triumphant look.

"Okay, hear us out…"

Uh oh, here we go.

"You know the perfect place to get over the sadness of losing a job?" Callie says.

"Uh. I don't know, a job fair?" I say, confused, half-joking but half-serious.

"No, silly! Paris!" Havannah exclaims, naming the city in her best French accent.

I sigh and make a face that communicates, *not this again.* I cross my arms and steel myself for battle.

"I already told you guys I can't go."

And I had told them that during our last girl's night when they'd tried to convince me taking this trip was a good idea.

A few girl's nights before that, I'd had a few too many glasses of champagne and let slip to Lina that going to Paris was my dream vacation. And who could blame me, right? I mean, we were watching *The*

Devil Wears Prada, and when Anne Hathaway got to go to Paris, it sort of spilled out of my mouth. I wasn't *actually* serious. But Lina has since taken it upon herself to make this trip happen, whether I want it to or not.

"Yeah, but that was before…when you were tied down to that hell hole of a job. You were worried about the time off, remember? Now you have it! It's the *perfect* time to go," Adelina says with a smile, as if she's delivered an epic closing argument.

She's not wrong. I don't have to worry about time off now. But, I do have to worry about spending an exorbitant amount of my savings while not bringing in any income.

"I don't want to burst anyone's bubble. I would love to go. But…it just doesn't make sense for me right now."

In an attempt to lighten the mood, before anyone can say anything, I blurt, "I mean…who would water my plants?!"

The girls laugh. "We can easily find someone to water your plants," Havannah says.

"We know you're not actually worried about your plants, Kai! Stop deflecting," Lina counters, a knowing smile aimed right at me.

"Plant," I correct, with an embarrassed laugh.

Truthfully, I only have one plant left after the others tragically died, and it's hanging on by a thread. Work had been pretty grueling lately, and my poor plant babies suffered. That, and I'm learning that maybe I don't have much of a green thumb.

"Okay, anyone else have any closing arguments before I deliver my verdict?" I say with a smirk.

"Uh oh, lawyer Kaia in the house," Callie says, feigning nervousness through a smile.

"Look, Kaia, I promise I'm not trying to force you into this. I think you *need* a break. You *need* to get away. This trip is for your own good, for crying out loud!" Adelina has started slowly shaking my shoulders back and forth.

Adelina's words reverberate in my mind. It's almost exactly what my mom told me. And if the people who know me best are saying these things to me… *maybe* I should listen. I haven't taken an actual vacation in who knows how long, and I've always wanted to go to Paris. So what exactly is holding me back from not taking this trip of a lifetime with my best girls? Not that I'd ever let them, but my parents did offer to pay my way, so money isn't really an issue. Plus I don't have a job, so I have *plenty* of time.

I've spent the last six years doing exactly what everyone expected of me. Somehow along the way I became the person that everyone leaned on when they needed something done, and I've taken it all in stride, without complaint.

Maybe…*maybe* it's time I did something for myself—something that isn't clearly marked on some perfectly curated plan for my life.

I've taken too long with my thoughts, and Lina must take my silence as an indication that I don't have anything further to say on the subject because she moves on.

"Okay, okay. No more Paris talk…" she starts as she lets go of my shoulders and grabs a handful of M&M's from a bowl on the counter. She walks back to the couch in the living room, adding "tonight" under her breath.

I can't help but steel myself to renew my arguments against going on this trip, but the longer I think through them, the less and less compelling they feel.

Once they've gone, I tidy up my apartment a bit,

then settle into bed with my computer to do some job searching and update my resume before I call it a night. Except somehow, I end up looking at flights to Paris instead of for open jobs.

I'm honestly not sure how I ended up here. My fingers have a mind of their own tonight. It's like I black out every time I end up on the job search engine and come to the booking page of a flight to Paris instead.

Sifting through my texts, I find Adelina's message with the proposed dates, a message I previously ignored.

I input the dates with shaky hands and watch as several flights pop up.

I scan them quickly and promptly close the browser.

Um, hello! Earth to Kaia! Focus on jobs, I think to myself.

I open the browser again and type in my job-searching platform of choice: Indeed. I resume my—admittedly boring—scroll through relevant jobs, saving the few that look semi-interesting.

I pause and open a new tab, almost without thinking, and begin typing in the same flight search engine I was using. My computer auto-fills the rest, taking me right to the same list of flights.

Flights I *shouldn't* be looking at because I'm not going to Paris.

I'm not going to Paris.

I click back over to Indeed and take a deep breath to focus my attention. *Jobs are good. And I need one. So this is what I need to be doing.* I silently will my brain to focus on what's important.

But…the other tab, only a click away, buzzes with possibility. *Why can't I just let this go?*

I click back over to the flight search engine and start scrolling again, delightfully surprised that they aren't as expensive as I expected.

I click on one and experience a rush of adrenaline. Joy. Excitement.

This is fun.

I'm staring at the total for a roundtrip flight to Paris, the proverbial edge of the slippery slope I'm currently on. A total I can absolutely afford right now, even given the fact that I'm unemployed.

Internally, I battle with myself about whether or not to go for it. Because who am I kidding? Everyone is right. I *want* to go to Paris, more than I want anything right now. A girl's trip to one of the most amazing cities in the entire world sounds like my dream vacation.

And I *need* a vacation.

I want a break, and at this point it's probably necessary to avoid crashing and burning in a fiery explosion of burnout.

Over the last several years, it's simply become so much easier to make the safe and practical choices. One of those was deciding that it wasn't the right time for this trip. But to be honest, I don't know when the right time is, or if I'll ever convince myself that the right time exists. So why not now?

I quickly enter my details and payment information for the tickets, pausing, letting my mouse hover over the button to complete the purchase. I quickly pull my hand away as if I've touched a hot stovetop.

No way. What am I doing? This feels reckless. I haven't even told the girls I'm slightly considering going on this trip. I should probably talk to them first, right?

I can hear Adelina now, telling me I should book them immediately and tell them later.

My hand drifts back to the mouse. Lightly. I tap

my finger on top of it a few times, until finally, I apply enough pressure to actually click it.

It's done.

Oh, god. It's happening.

Guess we're going to Paris.

CHAPTER 3: KAIA

"I can't believe we're going to Paris!" Callie says, face in her phone as she makes a list of all the places she wants to go on our first day there.

We're sitting in the airport terminal, absolutely buzzing with excitement about this trip. The girls still can't believe I changed my mind, and honestly? Neither can I. I partially blame sleep deprivation for this decision, my delirious alter-ego taking over my body and booking the tickets two months ago. Not to mention, I opted for the non-refundable tickets, so I must have been feeling a little reckless, and I knew I would back out if I had the option. So, I didn't give myself the option. And here we are.

Me: Um, I think I just booked

flights to Paris, but I'm not sure. I think I blacked out, my message to our group chat said.

OH MY GOSH, it's happening! Callie responded.

That's my girl. Booking mine now! Already have the webpage saved in my favorites. Adelina said.

Adelina is a freelance illustrator and never hesitates to book the vacation she's had her eyes on. "What's an artist to do but travel the world and gather inspiration for her work?" is her usual response when someone asks how she has the ability to travel so often. And gather inspiration, she does. Pretty much anywhere we go, Lina is inspired, and it's beautiful to witness. She finds a lot of the details most people don't, like the way the sun creates faint shadows on the side of a building, outlining nearby trees that blow in the wind. And it lights her up inside to be able to pull inspiration from so many beautiful places.

I'll double check I can get the studio covered for the trip, and then those tickets are all mine! Callie added.

She owns a pottery studio called *Seize The Clay*. She

makes the most beautiful bespoke pottery pieces, and also offers classes to those who want to learn. Her co-owner is a friend she met in college, and they run the studio as a dynamic duo. Thankfully, her partner was able to cover the studio for her so Callie could make the trip.

Havannah had responded about an hour later. Catching up on these! Just got out of a client meeting. C'est le moment de faire la fête—we're going to Paris!

Havannah is a nutritional therapist who focuses on disordered eating recovery. Her active clients were more than happy to complete their appointments virtually while she's in Paris, on the condition that she shares her view at least once during their session..

I zone back into the present, and my thoughts drift to dreamy, magical Paris. I don't think I can even begin to dream about all of the beautiful and amazing things we'll get to see and the food we're going to eat. I've heard the bread in Europe is about as good as it gets, so it will be carbs only on this trip, thank you very much.

I'm really excited, but anxiety lingers in the back

of my mind, ready to pounce at any given moment, threatening to ruin the trip entirely. I *can't* be the only one who obsesses about the worst case scenarios in any given situation.

I'm great. *Totally fine.* Excited and anxious. A good, healthy balance of joy and doom.

I look down at my phone to double—okay, triple—check the time. Thirty minutes until we board. *Should I go to the bathroom again? I think I need to grab another snack just in case.* I'm a nervous flier. I'm that girl who will get to the airport three hours early, make it through security in five minutes, grab a coffee, then sit at my gate…still worrying that I might somehow miss my flight.

"Did you just check the time again, Kai?" Adelina leans over and gives me a knowing smile.

"No," I deny. "Maybe I was checking to see if I had any text messages," I say with a defensive smile.

"Sure, sure." Her words are laced in sarcasm.

Sure enough, we board our flight seamlessly thirty minutes later, and there wasn't any need for my incessant worrying. Will that stop me from worrying the next time I step foot in an airport? Absolutely not.

In ten hours, we will be in Paris. The city of love, art, and culture—and I'm focusing solely on art and culture. No love for me.

I glance out the window during takeoff and watch my city get smaller and smaller, as my anticipation for the amazing adventure that awaits in France grows bigger and bigger.

The latte on the coffee table in front of me is the most amazing thing I've ever seen, rivaled only by the chocolate croissant delicately placed on the antique floral plate next to it.

"Wow, I've only been in Paris for—" Wait, how long have I been in Paris and why can't I remember?

Oh well. I'm in Paris, that's all that matters, right?

The first sip of my latte confirms it's as delicious as it looks. Decadent chocolate weaves through the strong but smooth nature of the French espresso, a dash of milk blending the two together seamlessly.

One word: *dreamy*.

Our Parisian villa overlooks a beautiful garden with views of the city beyond. I'm still in shock we scored such an incredible Airbnb, but I am overjoyed to call this place home for a few weeks.

Cabinets opening and dishes moving in the next room pull my attention back inside, and I internally squeal. *Eeek, the girls must be awake!* Time for a day of Parisian exploring and shopping.

"Hey! How'd you sleep?" I call.

"Great, babe—how about you?" The response does not come in the voice of one of my friends. That was the sound of an adult man. A stranger. Someone who shouldn't be in my Airbnb right now. *And…* did he call me babe?

Immediately, I'm searching for anything I can use to defend myself.

C'mon, Kaia, you've watched enough true crime to know what to do, right?

Turns out, I'm not as mentally prepared as I thought I'd be should I ever have to fight for my life.

A purple geode acting as a paperweight sits on the table, and I arm myself with it before rising and tiptoeing toward the kitchen.

I stop right before the entrance and take a deep breath.

Before I can lose my nerve, I round the corner, holding the geode high in the air, letting out what was supposed to be a battle cry, but came out more like a terrified cow. I'll let you use your imagination on that one.

I freeze as I enter the room and drop my makeshift weapon immediately out of pure shock. I can't believe what I'm seeing—like it's actually not registering in my brain.

I take a couple of steps back and look around to orient myself. I look back at the man standing in front of me, blinking an aggressive amount of times, sure that something is wrong with my eyes.

The man on the other end of the mystery voice coming from the kitchen, the man standing in front of me, is Jon Bernthal. My celebrity crush, Jon Bernthal. As in, *The Punisher*, Jon Bernthal. And he's looking at me like I'm an absolute crazy person—not that I can blame him after I just rushed him with a sparkly rock.

"Kaia?" he says, confusion registering on his face, but he sounds like he's underwater.

Am I dying? How does he know my name?

"Kaia!" he says again, but this time, his voice is a lot higher and the room blurs.

Oh god, I am dying. It's happening. I'm having a

stroke or something.

"Kai, wake up." My body jolts upward, and I smack my head on something cold and hard.

Realization hits me harder. Dreamland is fading and reality settles in its place.

I'd fallen asleep in my seat…on an airplane to Paris, France.

"Some dream you were having, huh?" I look up to see Callie smiling down at me.

"Look! We're here!" she squeals with excitement, pointing out the window toward the city beneath us.

The smell of fresh coffee fills the room as I open the French doors off the living room in my dream apartment, which I get to call home for the next four weeks. The *real* Parisian apartment, not the one from my strange Jon Bernthal dream yesterday. This one looks nothing like the one from my dream, but it's equally as beautiful, and much better because it's real. And I never want to leave. The walls are painted a beautiful eggshell, and it makes the forest green velvet couch in the living room shine like it's the star of the show. The fresh peonies on the counter in the kitchen are in full bloom, a kind gift left by the Airbnb hosts.

People speaking French at a nearby cafe floats through the window, creating melodic background noise that becomes the soundtrack of my slow morning, the pale pink linen curtains blowing in the wind, almost as if they're dancing to the sound of the city below.

We've been here for twenty-four hours, and Paris is already the most inspiring place I've ever been—full of beautiful and interesting people and the most incredible bread. *Oh my god, the bread.* Our very first stop when we got into the city was a cafe. We didn't even drop our suitcases off first. We were starving, and in desperate need of caffeine. After finally checking into our place, we spent the next eight hours sleeping, because not even our lattes and cappuccinos could counteract the jet lag.

Waking up this morning, I'm still not convinced this isn't a dream. I give myself a playful pinch on the arm. *Nope, this is real life.* Swirls of steam escaping from the French press remind me that my daily cup of "I'm a functioning human" juice —a.k.a. my beloved cup of morning coffee—is ready, which is also ten times better in Paris, I might add. I open the antique hutch in the kitchen, home to an eclectic handmade mug collection, and pull out the one in front. I pour my coffee into a bright orange mug, donning the words "c'est la vie" hand painted on the front in pink lettering.

We don't have concrete plans today—only to explore Paris like locals, and I can't wait. It feels like there's so much potential for adventure and inspiration here.

I make my way back to the room I'm sharing with Havannah and start getting ready for the day. I've opted for a white linen jumpsuit with a plain white tank underneath. Will I regret wearing all white today? Probably. But I'll consider it an Olympic-level feat if I make it through the day without spilling on myself.

I hear Adelina and Callie getting up, and I get even more excited to get the day started and get out of the Airbnb.

Havannah got up early and went for a run, and got back only a few minutes ago. I should've followed her lead this morning for some extra exploring time and movement after our long travel day, but then I'd have to get out of bed earlier than I wanted to. And then I'd have to run. *Need I say more?*

"Be ready in twenty?" Callie calls out from the other room.

"You bet!" I shout back.

I sit on the floor on my side of the bed and quickly do my makeup in the beautiful antique floor mirror in our room. It's gold but tarnished, giving it that perfect vintage look. It's amazing, and I'm sort of wondering if I can find one like it here in town and what I need to do to fit it in my suitcase.

I know it's not possible, but a girl can dream, right?

We shuffle around each other getting ready—borrowing and lending each other clothes, purses, and shoes, until we're each fully satisfied with the outfit we've chosen for a day of magical exploration and a lot of pictures.

Our first stop is a cafe down the street from our Airbnb. We all opt for the traditional Parisian breakfast—a croissant and a coffee. The best croissant and coffee I've ever had, I should add. The coffee was smooth and rich, and that's saying a lot for me because I rarely enjoy the taste of coffee. And the croissant…don't get me started on the croissant. Buttery and flaky goodness all rolled into a beautiful, hand-held masterpiece.

I'm already blown away, and we've only gone two blocks from our flat.

We're all sitting inside at a cafe table, and I notice that the barista—correction, the Greek-god—at the counter has been looking at our table on and off for the past couple of minutes. More specifically, he's looking at Callie. She, of course, is oblivious, but I've noticed.

"Pssst…" I say to her, nudging her with my elbow, "don't look now because you'll make it obvious, but the cute barista has been checking you out for the past ten minutes."

She immediately looks up and locks eyes with Mr. Handsome in an awkward but adorable moment. They both quickly look away at the same time, and we all giggle to ourselves.

"I told you *not* to look!" I laugh, keeping my voice low.

"Sorry, I panicked!" Callie throws her palm to her face in embarrassment.

"Umm, I don't know about you, but I could feel the sparks from here when you guys made eye contact," Havannah says.

"Oh, please." Callie rolls her eyes and sneaks another glance over her shoulder. He's turned around to work on the espresso machine.

"No, she's right—I saw it too!" Adelina says.

"Agreed!" I say enthusiastically.

"What do I do? It's not like I can give him my number… right?" she asks, half-excited, half-concerned.

Havannah reaches into her purse and rips off the end of a receipt she had floating around. "Anyone have a pen?" she asks.

"Oooh, I do!" Adelina says excitedly.

Adelina hands her the pen, and Havannah scribbles down Callie's phone number.

She slides it in her direction. "We're in Paris, Callie! Give the cute guy your number. You never know what'll happen."

Callie looks down at the piece of paper and smiles as she grabs it. "You know what? You're right. Wish me luck!" She hesitates before pushing her chair out, standing and confidently strolling away, turning back to give us an excited smile before approaching the counter.

"Ah, they grow up so fast," Adelina says jokingly,

and we all giggle quietly.

I quietly whisper, "Go, Callie, go!"

Honestly, I'm so proud of her—already taking risks and living life to the fullest. I hope I learn to do the same while I'm here.

Callie comes back to the table, giddy and buzzing with excitement and nervous energy.

"So, how'd it go? When's the wedding?" I ask.

She laughs and playfully swats at my arm.

"His name is Jules, and he's very sweet. A little shy, which I like," she gushes. She's smitten. The pink in her cheeks is a dead giveaway.

"He also…gave me his number and said to text him anytime," she adds quickly, trying to gloss over it like that isn't the best part of their whole conversation.

Adeline squeals in excitement.

"Shhhh!" Callie says. "I don't want him to think I'm a weird super fan!" Callie starts laughing, and we all join in until our stomachs hurt and tears roll down our faces.

I pull back and take a moment to appreciate the fact that I'm here, with my best friends, having the time of my life.

These are the good old days, and I promise myself I won't rush past them because this trip is slightly outside of my comfort zone.

I'm going to savor *every single moment.*

CHAPTER 4: KAIA

We ended up in *Le Marais* for a day of Parisian thrifting. How do you say "living the dream" in French? Because that's how I feel today. With second coffees in hand, we're ready to shop until we drop.

First stop? An *adorable* shop with a hot pink awning. We step inside, and I take it all in. There are racks and racks of vintage clothing—some hidden gems, and others that should stay hidden, but that's a typical thrifting trip.

I leave with a vintage tee—my go to thrift score. It's so faded that I can't actually tell what's on the front, but it has an almost tie-dye design right in the middle and it's perfectly oversized, so I couldn't leave without it. And I will probably wear it every day for the next week. We each leave the shop with a hot pink bag holding our treasures, and I pause outside to take a photo of the matching bag and awning.

"I have a vintage furniture shop on my must see list, and it's a pretty short walk," Havannah says. "Can we head there next?"

"Onward!" Callie calls, thrusting her fist in the air.

We spend the morning strolling through the beautiful streets, practically skipping because we're so giddy. I'm in awe as we walk. How can a city be this beautiful? Not only the cobblestones, or the architecture, but the people—so many *beautiful* people. And they're so *fashionable*. I consider myself relatively fashionable according to Pacific Northwest standards, but my Target shoes are nothing compared to these designer-looking flats, heels, and fancy sneakers I see walking through the streets of Paris.

I mean, no offense, Target. I'll love you forever, and you're perfect just the way you are.

After all of our walking this morning, we decide to stop by a darling-looking crepe cart and pick up a snack. I went for the lemon sugared one, Adelina and Callie opted for strawberry, and Havannah got the Nutella. I'm pretty sure lemon sugar is my new love language.

The next few minutes are spent walking in silence, except for the occasional hum of pleasure that comes from eating these delicious crepes. We're trekking our way to our next stop, about a fifteen minute walk from the crepe cart. When the phone signals our arrival, we all look up to a beautiful cream building. It looks like an old home that's been converted into a shop. It has two small white-paned windows on the storefront and large flower pots sitting on the ground under each, adorned in colorful blooms. I'm no floral expert, but I recognize the peonies at least. The front door is painted a beautiful, muted yellow with a charming *bienvenue* sign.

A bell chimes over the door as we walk in. The shop is much bigger than it looks from the outside, going as far back as the eye can see, and I noticed upon first glance that there seems to be a downstairs as well.

"Bonjour, mes dames!" A woman says from the corner. She's fluffing a couple of pastel blue pillows on a cream chair near one of the front windows. She has a very chic short bob and a yellow silk scarf that matches the front door tied around her neck.

Can she adopt me and pass her perfect Parisian style on to me, please?

"*Bonjour!*" we all parrot back.

It has a maximalist sort of vibe, with amazing items sitting from floor to ceiling, styled beautifully, of course. Everywhere you look, there are trinkets, art, pieces of furniture, books, and more. My eyes can't possibly take in everything, though not for lack of trying as I scan the shelves and furniture. They catch on a particular shelf displaying what looks to be a vase made to look like a book. I walk over to inspect it further and see that the outside is a light blue, adorned in intricate hand painted swirls in a canary yellow, complemented by florals in various shades of pink. The text on the front reads "*la fleur fleurira si tu la laisses faire,*" and I take a picture of it so I can look up the translation later. I run my fingers over the details, admiring the craftsmanship, before carefully setting it back on the shelf. I could *probably* fit it in my suitcase, but I wouldn't want to risk it breaking. Not to mention, the room I allotted myself for souvenirs is dwindling *quickly*. If it wasn't strange to high-five yourself in public—or in private for that matter—I'd give myself one in celebration for having the willpower to leave that beautiful vase behind.

I turn to meet with the girls, who've migrated to the next room in the shop. This might sound dramatic, but being here almost brings me to tears. All my thrift girlies know, a good thrift day with your best friends is a spiritual experience. Throw Paris into the mix, and it's my favorite day ever.

We end up spending over an hour exploring every inch of our new favorite store in Paris, and while there is no shortage of beautiful and unique treasures to be found there, the only thing we ended up leaving with is a dainty piece of jewelry each.

Once I discovered the jewelry section, I knew I couldn't possibly walk out of here without purchasing something. The pieces were displayed on an antique writer's desk, each drawer pulled out and lined with various floral scarves, jewelry artfully placed on top. To the antique-uninterested eye, this desk might've looked like a piece of junk better suited for the side of the road with a "FREE" sign on front, but not to me. This desk is a piece of art—covered in a creamy paint, chipped in all the right places. Dents and scrapes told the mysterious stories of words that were written at this desk. Poetry, perhaps. Grocery lists, I'm sure. Novels, maybe. All I know is it was well-used and well-loved. And now it's home to an amazing collection of dainty jewelry.

I found a ring that spoke to me. It's a true yellow gold, with a braided band and a tiny gem on the top. Havannah decided—after debating for ten minutes between two pieces—on a gold necklace with a gem star in the center. Callie chose a dainty cuff bracelet with the phrase *"chacun voit midi à sa porte"* engraved on the inside, which we learned is a French proverb that translates to "everyone sees noon at his own door." Essentially, it means that everyone sees things their own way. Adelina left with a pair of beautiful silver huggie earrings. After paying, we all donned our jewelry on our way out of the store, and I was so glad to have a fun tangible reminder of this day, this trip with my best friends.

As we walk down the street, our next destination unknown, I notice a tattoo shop. An idea swiftly travels from my brain and out of my mouth before I can even consider it.

"We have to get tattoos while we're here," I say.

Havannah whirls around to look at me, wearing possibly the biggest smile I've ever seen. I know I'm speaking her language when I talk about tattoos; she's got at least fifteen, mostly dainty ones spanning her hands and arms.

"Don't tempt me with a good time," she says.

I take approximately ten seconds to reconsider then say, "I'm serious, let's do it!"

Havannah jumps up and down excitedly, and Lina and Callie look at me with a mix of amusement and disbelief.

"Kai, this might be the best idea you've ever had." Havannah squeezes me into a hug.

"I don't know whether I should thank you or if I'm offended," I say as I squeeze her back.

"I'm way too sober to get a tattoo right this second, but I'm adding it to our shared list of excursions," Callie says, a disbelieving smile peeking over her phone as she types away.

"Deal!" Havannah squeals.

We walk past the tattoo parlor…for now. As we continue down the street, I am so content in a way I haven't been in a long time. I'm in *Paris* with my best friends, and I'm ready to see what this city has to offer me.

"I'll take the spaghetti à la bolognaise, *s'il vous plaît*," I say to the kind server taking our order at *Le Chat Noir*, a popular restaurant near the *Moulin Rouge*. The restaurant is dimly lit, and very avant-garde, with red pleather booths and art covering every wall.

We're all tired from an amazing, but long day, and I couldn't be more excited to enjoy some fresh pasta and a glass of red wine before we head back to our comfy Parisian home.

After a quiet dinner and paying our check, we convinced the server to snap a couple of pictures of us at our table to commemorate our spectacular day in Paris—one of us and one with him making a surprise cameo.

People can say what they want about Parisians, but every single person I've met has been incredibly kind to us.

"Let's stop by the *Moulin Rouge* on our way out!" Callie urges us as we make our way out of the restaurant.

Thanks to the delicious dinner or the red wine, we all seem to have found a second wind, so we walk down the street to the *Moulin Rouge* for some sightseeing, with no actual plans to go inside. While the *Moulin Rouge* is smaller in person than I thought it would be, I'm still taken aback by it's allure and flashing lights. We find ourselves posing for more pictures with the giant red windmill as our backdrop.

Standing in the iconic spot with my best friends, I feel alive, inspired, and buzzing with joy. *I may never leave. This is home now.* I catch myself smiling at the thought.

"Let's go grab a drink!" one of the girls says, and my buzz dissipates. I'm tired and was looking forward to curling up on the couch with my book.

Havannah is pointing toward a little nondescript Irish pub on the opposite side of the *Moulin Rouge*. I hadn't even noticed it, but of course Havannah did. As much as I love a pub—I'm a pub girl, not a club girl—I was really ready to change out of this dress and into my comfy clothes.

I look at the pub and back over to the girls, brows furrowed, letting out a small groan.

"C'mon! It'll just be *one* beer," Callie says.

Yeah, I've heard that one before.

"An hour *tops*!" Havannah chimes in.

I put on my best thinking face, tapping my chin, as I pretend I have any real say in the matter. All three of them stare at me with their best puppy dog eyes, and I don't have it in me to squash their excitement. Our comfy night at home will just have to wait.

"Ok, *fine*. I'm in," I say as I loop my arm through Callie's and pull her toward the front door. "For *one* beer. I'm serious."

"Mhm, yep. One beer." Her agreeing nod is over-exaggerated, and her sly smile gives me no confidence that I'll be out of this dress and in my bed any time soon.

The pub is dimly lit, but my eyes adjust quickly as we walk in. It's not too busy, and the vibe seems pretty chill, with low music playing in the background and groups of people bunched in corners chatting loudly over their drinks. This might not have been my first choice of activities, but if I *have* to be out, this atmosphere is pretty ideal. We head to the bar and each order a beer.

We've been there about ten minutes, not even halfway through our drinks, when out of the corner of my eye, I see a man walking toward us at the bar and immediately regret coming here.

Which is not this man's fault. I was simply hoping to grab a drink with my friends then head back to the Airbnb for a relaxing night. What I wasn't prepared to do tonight was socialize in a pub, yelling my name ten times to the stranger in front of me because they couldn't hear it over the cacophony of fun being had by everyone else around me.

I sip my beer and look down at my glass as the guy approaches, hoping I can just mind my business until the coast is clear. Someone taps me on the shoulder. I look up and make eye contact with a strikingly handsome man. He's literally the picturesque definition of tall, dark, and handsome. His hair is a deep, chocolate brown, making his blue eyes pop in contrast. He's wearing a white button-down shirt, slacks, and Chelsea boots. I think that's a Rolex around his wrist, and I find myself curious to know what this guy does for a living that he can afford one…not that it's any of my business. I catch a whiff of his cologne. I'm not sure what it is, but it's nice— woodsy, with a slight hint of vanilla.

After a mere moment of taking in the presence of this man, I notice his hand is extended, holding a rose made out of a napkin in *my* direction. When I look up again, his mouth curls into a soft smile, growing as my attention focuses on the small scar over his top lip. I blink and quickly look away, giving him an apologetic smile. He nods toward the rose, and I take it from him, nodding and smiling in nonverbal thanks. Neither of us said a word, but somehow the moment didn't feel as awkward as it should've. It was sweet.

I watch discreetly as he walks back to the booth in the far corner of the pub, where he sits with two other men. One of them gives him what they assume is a subtle high five, but I can confirm it was about as subtle as a firework.

I giggle, my cheeks warming with a blush, and turn to my friends, twirling the rose in my fingertips.

"Okay, that was *the* sweetest! Are you going to go talk to him?" Callie asks.

"No, no. It was very sweet, but I'm here for a girl's night! No boys allowed," I joke and nudge her playfully.

I'm not looking for anything remotely close to romance on this trip. No way, no how. *Not gonna happen, bucko.*

"Speak for yourself," says Adelina, staring in the

distance with a dreamy expression on her face. "French men are hot, and I wouldn't be mad if I got an *adorable* napkin rose from one of them." She nods her head toward where Napkin Rose Guy is sitting with his friends.

That's what we're calling him now since I'm not planning to ask him what his name is—Napkin Rose Guy.

"Here, you can have it. Your dream come true," I say, handing her the rose with an overly enthusiastic smile on my face.

We all laugh as she swats my hand away.

I finish the rest of my second beer—we all knew it was never going to be just one—and close out my tab with the bartender. We've been sitting at the bar in the pub for about forty minutes, and we're all feeling ready to head back to our place for the night.

"Ready to head out?" asks Callie.

I put my finger up, a gesture for them to wait for just a minute.

"I need to do something real quick."

I'm not sure if it was the tiny boost of courage

from the two beers I had or the fear of looking like a jerk for not saying anything in the first place, but I have to go thank Napkin Rose Guy for the sweet gesture before we leave.

I walk toward their table shyly, the three men marking my every move. I'm immediately drawn to the sandy-haired man on the right. His eyes catch mine, and I forget what I came over to say. They're a really beautiful mix of hazel and green that matches the rather form-fitting long-sleeve shirt hugging his muscular arms in a way that isn't difficult to look at. His sandy hair is artfully messed up. His face is a little pink in all the areas the sun hits, like he spends a lot of time outside. And his smile. Wow, his smile. It lights up his whole face, and maybe the whole room.

Oh boy. I need to say thank you and get the heck out of here before I fall in love with a man I'm never going to see again.

I lean over to Napkin Rose Guy and, with my best French accent, say "*Merci!*"

"Oh, you're welcome!"

I had turned to walk away but stop.

"Wait…you speak English?" I ask when I turn back.

"*You* speak English?" he says back, his words heavily accented.

I wager a guess. "Australia?"

"America?"

I laugh. "That's me."

"Just a couple of Aussies, here!" the one on the left chimes with a heart stopping crooked smile and a wink. I can't help but notice that his biceps are also the circumference of my thigh.

"Well, thank you again," I say to Napkin Rose Guy. "This was very sweet of you. Enjoy your night." I wave as I head toward the exit where the girls are waiting for me.

"Wait, wait…you're leaving already?" Napkin Rose Guy jumps up, excitement in his voice. "I'm Lachlan, by the way, but everyone just calls me Lach."

I can't deny it. He's incredibly handsome, and charming—which is a combination I'm not sure I want anything to do with right now.

"Nice to meet you, Lachlan. I'm Kaia," I say as the girls approach; I'm sure they were dying to know what was being said over here.

"I'm Adelina." Lina smiles and crosses her ankles, something she does when she's either nervous or excited.

He chuckles, his pearly white teeth flashing in this dimly lit pub. "Lachlan. It's a pleasure, ladies."

"This is Havannah and Callie." I point to the girls as they give a quick wave. I do a double take and catch the day-dreamy look on Havannah's face, immediately knowing we're not going home anytime soon.

The other two guys with Lachlan get up to introduce themselves.

"I'm Angus! Glad you ladies are here to liven up the evening," says the mountain of a man standing to the left of Lachlan. He points to each of us and tries to recall all of our names— which he does so correctly. *Impressive.*

"Hey, I'm Jack," the one who was sitting to the right of Lachlan, the one I was first drawn to when I approached their table, gives a quick nod and a devastatingly handsome grin. Without a shadow of a doubt, I know I need to stay away from him.

"These are my best mates," Lachlan says, throwing an arm around each of the guys' necks. "I've been scoping out some office space for a Paris branch of my company, and these guys love a free trip, so here we are."

Okay, so he owns his own company *and* he's looking for space for a Paris branch? Explains the Rolex.

"Amazing!" Havannah practically drools. "We're here on a girl's trip!"

"We've been dreaming of this trip for years and we *finally* booked it," Callie says, bumping my hip with hers.

"Girl's trip, eh?" Lachlan's ocean-blue eyes twinkle with amusement.

"Oh, *and* we're here to celebrate Kaia getting out of a toxic situation and finding her happiness again!" Adelina adds, shooting me a look as if to remind me that I'm here to have fun and not worry so much. *Darn her. She knows me too well.*

I know she only wants me to remember that it's okay to let loose and have fun, but I am completely out of my element in this situation.

"That's right!" I give a thumbs up to the group, immediately regretting it.

Can we please rewind time to before the awkward hijacked my body?

Lachlan laughs and nudges my shoulder. "I like you guys! I reckon our night just got much better

Now, let's get you girls a drink."

CHAPTER 5: KAIA

As fate would have it, these guys are actually really fun to hang out with. When they asked us to stay and have a drink with them, I thought for sure we were living the beginning of a *Taken* movie, but so far, so good. We've been hanging out with them for over two hours and seemed to have skipped over the awkward small talk phase of friendship and right into the good stuff. Lachlan, Jack, and Angus have been perfect gentlemen all evening, and though I'm apprehensive to admit it, I don't think this will be the last night we spend time with them during this trip.

Lachlan, otherwise known as Napkin Rose Guy, is easily the extrovert of the group. He has a commanding presence about him. Not in a negative way, but in a way that makes you want to be in his orbit. It could be his charming smile accentuating the small scar above his mouth, or his careless attitude, but whatever it is, he's got the eye of most girls in this place. I can imagine some people might think he's arrogant, but my guess is he lacks a bit of self-awareness.

Not to mention, he's the definition of tall, dark, and handsome, and Havannah has definitely taken notice of that. I hold back a giggle at the memory of the look on her face when she officially met him. She was the human version of the heart-eye emoji, and it was the cutest thing I've ever seen. He introduced himself and nudged her arm with his, complimenting her "rad name" in the process. She usually gets compliments on her name when people meet her for the first time, but the look on her face when Lachlan spoke told me that his compliment was her favorite in a while.

Angus, the resident goof ball of the group, is *hilarious*. I can't remember the last time I held-my-sides-because-I-ran-out-of-breath laughed so hard, but Angus is talented. He's also deeply kind—asking genuine questions and listening with care. I'd like to meet his parents simply so I can thank them for raising such a wonderful guy. If I had to guess, I'd say he's at least six-foot-three, and he has the stature of a pro wrestler. He's a former professional rugby player, and he definitely looks the part, though he coaches now. Currently, he's singing "Don't Stop Believing" on the karaoke machine across the pub. He's got quite an audience of people, all jumping, dancing, singing along with his terrible, but entertaining, rendition of the classic song. His seemingly choreographed dance moves earn him extra points with this crowd tonight. They're cheering him on as if they're actually watching Journey live, and not a drunk Australian rugby player with an affinity for karaoke after one too many beers.

I look away from Angus to find Lachlan and Jack doing some sort of secret handshake to the beat of the song. They're laughing and jumping around, completing a random and ridiculous series of hand and feet movements, almost perfectly in sync. I'm laughing so hard that tears are forming when my eyes focus on Jack, and the way his muscles ripple through his shirt with every movement.

Ah, yes, Jack. He's the quietest one of the three of

them, but not in the sense that he's shy. I get the feeling he doesn't say anything he doesn't mean, and he doesn't talk only to fill the air with words. The intentional way he speaks intrigues me. In fact, pretty much everything about Jack intrigues me, which might explain why I've been gravitating toward him all evening. Not that it matters, because he's been talking to everyone but me tonight, except for when he introduced himself.

I glance over at him and can't help but appreciate how incredibly good looking he is. His sandy brown hair complements his green eyes perfectly. His scoop-neck, olive, long-sleeve shirt hugs his toned biceps, revealing his tattoos where the sleeves are bunched at his elbows. I resist the urge to study each one from here.

I blink quickly, coming back from the ridiculous trance I was in, practically drooling over handsome Jack.

And I make a mental note to never call him that again. "Heya, mate!" Angus says, surprising me when he returns from the stage and throws his arm around my shoulders, pulling me in for a side hug. He's so much taller than me, the top of my head fits right in the crook of his arm.

We're on our second round of tequila shots, after who knows how many beers and one round of cosmos—suggested by Angus, funnily enough. The nightly rush has hit the pub, the space filling with energetic locals and tourists alike. Thankfully, the guys secured the booth in the corner early in the evening, and we've been chatting and dancing the night away without being bothered too much by the masses.

"Guys, did you see the photo booth?" Callie throws her arms around mine and Havannah's shoulders, leaning her weight heavily on us, and I sense she might not have needed that second tequila shot. "C'mon, we have to go take some pics before it gets any more packed in here!" she adds.

"Okay, okay—let's go," I say, pulling Adelina away from the conversation she's having with Angus.

"We'll be back!" Havannah says, waving to Lachlan as we push our way through the pulsing crowd toward the photo booth.

The rest of the night is a little bit of a blur, but an incredibly fun blur nonetheless. The girls and I "absolutely crushed" the photo booth, according to an adorable intoxicated Callie. I stare down at the strip of pictures in my hand. In all four pictures, at least one of us is out of frame, and none of us could hold our planned poses long enough without laughing, so they're all slightly blurry. I smile at the photos, tucking them away in my purse. They're perfect. These friends of mine are perfect. Dare I say, this night is…perfect?

Definitely *not* the alcohol talking.

I pull out my phone to check the time, grateful my it's still in my possession, and I swear the numbers lighting up my screen are running away from me. It takes me a couple seconds to accurately read the time. Fifteen minutes past midnight.

"Almost time to call it night, gals?"

I lean in and clink my glass against Adelina's in a small cheers. She doesn't respond to me, but the way her head slowly bobs off beat to the music tells me she's more than ready. We're sitting at the bar, leaving the guys to hang back at the booth for a bit. Havannah's been chatting with the bartender for a couple minutes. They both have small sparrow tattoos on their wrist, and have been bonding over their love for quality, craft cocktail making, swapping names of their favorite Instagram accounts and blogs.

I lean forward to ask Callie if she's ready to head home soon, and out of the corner of my eye, I see Havannah get onto the bar top. I turn toward her, eyes-wide but not fully surprised. I've been out with Havannah a multitude of times, and this move is so very *her*. I'm about to try and coax her down when I realize her new bartender bff is helping her over to the other side of the bar. Within twenty seconds, she has a cocktail shaker in her hand.

I pull out my phone and snap a few pictures.

This is amazing, I think to myself, then wonder, *And also…is this allowed?*

I watch in awe as Havannah makes a beautiful, pink-colored cocktail like an absolute professional and slides in down to a guy sitting a couple stools over from us. He nods in thanks, and she looks to the bartender for her next assignment.

Someone slides onto the stool next to me, the one Havannah *was* sitting on, and I turn to find Angus smiling down at me, Lachlan and Jack behind him, each leaning over one of his shoulders.

"How's it going, ladies? Where's the fourth

musketeer?" Angus asks, obviously missing Havannah with a hand on her hip, smirking at him from behind the bar. Lachlan laughs as soon as he notices and taps Angus on the shoulder, directing his attention toward her.

"Woah, mate!" Angus lets out a bellowing laugh and leans forward. "Does this mean the rest of our drinks are free?"

The bartender heard that one. "Absolutely not!" She glances our way with a knowing smile. "However, Irish car bombs on me if you guys wanna play a little game."

"You're on!" Lachlan shouts at the bartender, almost before she can even finish her sentence. Apparently, Lachlan is game for *anything*, especially when drinks are involved.

As she gets the drinks ready, the boys look more excited than I've seen them all night. More excited than when we ordered a large basket of cheese fries and wings. Angus is fake stretching, and Lachlan and Jack are looking at each other like they've been on rival sports teams their entire lives. It's as if the bartender asked them to compete in the Olympics or something; they're so into it. Callie, Adelina, and I watch them, thoroughly entertained, as the bartender sets three Irish car bombs in front of them. She repeats the super complicated instructions of the game: *finish your drink before your opponent.*

"You're on, mates."

I turn to see Jack shoot his friends a challenging look before readying his hand on his glass. This is the closest I've been to him all night, earning me a front row seat to his smile, and it may just be my undoing. My heart is silently cheering him on if it means he'll keep smiling like that.

"Ready?" The bartender holds a towel up like a flag. "Set..."

The boys are intensely concentrated on the bartender's go-ahead, waiting for the magic word. No one in our group moves or makes a sound, all watching intently like this is the most important sporting event we'll ever witness.

"GO!"

CHAPTER 6: JACK

"Oi! Another round, mates?" Lachlan is already four beers and at least two tequila shots deep at this point, so he doesn't consider his volume. I'm surprised there are people in the bar who haven't turned our way with how he's yelling and carrying on.

"I'm set," I say, leaning closer to him. He pretends like he can't hear me and makes his way to the bar. I was pretty buzzed *before* we chugged those Irish car bombs, so I'm definitely feeling it now. To no one's surprise, Angus won the little game. I was pretty close, though. If Lachlan wasn't already sloshed at that point, he might've stood a chance.

"He's pissed," I mutter to Angus.

This isn't new behavior for Lachlan. In fact, it's

because of his antics that the three of us are mates at all, thanks to the World Cup five years ago and a bar that looked remarkably like this one.

I'll leave the rest to your imagination.

Angus shrugs and continues tapping his foot to the music pumping through the speakers, then turns to talk to Callie. Or is that one Havannah? I should at least pretend to be paying better attention.

We've spent the last few hours with these four girls and, if I'm being honest, it wasn't how I pictured our night going. To be fair, it's hard to have a clear picture of an evening out with Lachlan because literally anything can happen. I've got a scar and two police reports that prove it. I'm not upset about them joining us at the booth, but I'm not exactly letting my enjoyment show either.

I've been told in the past I'm hard to read, but I prefer it that way, and I think Lachlan does, too. He means well, but he's got a larger-than-life personality that stems from some trauma and a deep desire to be loved. But the man's got a heart of gold, and he'd do just about anything for me and Angus—including trying to improve our evening with the company of these girls.

When they walked into the pub, they had more than enough attention. But Lachlan is not one to be outdone. He watched the girls sit down and immediately "staked his claim"—his words, not mine —on the red head wearing the converse and a white dress. The dress hits right above her knees, and I immediately wish I didn't recall that detail.

I don't know who he felt like he needed to "stake a claim" from anyway. Angus is more than happy with his girl back home and I'm, well…I'm not looking for *anything* right now.

For Lachlan, since the reason we're in Paris is for him and his business, I try putting on an expression that hopefully makes me look interested and entertained.

I want him to have a good trip, and I'm willing to do just about anything to make that happen, hence being in a pub for the fifth night in a row. I'd do anything, that is, except drinking the shot he's undoubtedly going to peer pressure me into drinking in five seconds.

"For my best mate." He extends the shot in my direction and bats his eyelashes for good measure.

"Sure, Lach, but only because I love you." I put

the glass to my lips and watch as he turns away, satisfied. Then, I gently set the full shot glass onto the table, knowing someone in our party will put it to good use.

"Alright, you sneak. You can't make me be the only one who takes shots with Lach tonight," Angus says, leaning over hitting his shoulder with mine.

This mountain of man knocks me sideways harder than he intended, and I'm sure it has *nothing* to do with the shots. Angus doesn't have an aggressive bone in his body—unless we're on the rugby pitch.

I let out a laugh. "Someone has to be responsible tonight."

Angus shrugs and picks up the shot intended for me. I knew it wouldn't go to waste.

Who am I kidding? I'm always the responsible one. I'm not saying that's all by choice, but when you're friends with a guy like Lachlan, you need to have someone in your party with their guard up, or you might wind up stranded on a roof in Brisbane with a dog whose name you don't know.

It's been a good long while since I've actually let loose.

I run my eyes over the group, ensuring everyone is

accounted for, and I lock eyes with Kaia.

It's hard to tell in the dim lighting of the pub, but her eyes are like the exact shade of mahogany.

I don't know how long we stay like this, and I can't remember the last time I took a breath, but what I know is that she is stunning. It crosses my mind that Lachlan made his interest in her very clear, so I'm the first to look away.

I noticed her the second she walked in. She didn't see me, but I saw her, auburn hair swinging in her high ponytail as she leaned across the bar to order, her dress climbing the back of her thighs in a way that made me plant my feet more firmly into the ground. But what caught me was her smile. When I saw her smile at the bartender, it was genuine, as if she couldn't be happier to be here. The kind of smile that makes your cheeks hurt if you wear it for too long.

Then she and her friends joined our party, or I guess I should say Lachlan's orbit. It's hard not to get caught up in him, with his tall frame and dark hair. The man's got charisma when he's not under the influence of half a bottle of tequila.

And there's Kaia standing next to him. She has this

sort of quiet, natural beauty about her. Nothing in your face or overdone.

I've been keeping to myself most of the night, responding when asked the basic getting-to-know-a-stranger-in-a-bar questions, enjoying seeing Lachlan in his element. I'm content to be here, observing rather than engaging.

As if I can't help myself, I glance at Kaia again. She's twirling the napkin rose Lachlan gave her, and I let a small smile loose. She really is beautiful. And in that moment, I find myself wishing I didn't think so, but I do. Or rather, wishing I didn't know. Thinking implies opinion, and her beauty far outweighs opinion. It's a fact. I would be hard-pressed to find anyone who didn't think she was beautiful. But in the last few covert glances, I've noticed a hint of sadness underneath that beauty, and I want to learn more about it. I find myself wanting to protect her from whatever makes her sad, do whatever it takes to keep that breathtaking smile on her face.

I raise my beer bottle to my lips and take a sip, letting go of my curiosity about Kaia. I glance over at Angus instead, only to find he's already staring at me. A sly smile spreads across his face, and he shakes his head slowly, as if he knows some big secret about me.

"What?" I say, unimpressed, bottle still to my lips.

"You got it bad, mate. It's written all over your face."

Lowering my bottle, I keep my face carefully blank of any emotion.

"I've got nothing."

"Oh, no. You've got it *real* bad"

I roll my eyes and take another, albeit large, sip of my beer, and Angus chuckles to himself.

The moment I step out of the loo, I'm immediately concerned, because I don't see Lachlan anywhere. The second thing I feel is ice cold liquid seeping through my shirt. Confused and wet, I look up to meet the eyes of the girl I've been actively avoiding but thinking about all night.

I was right. Mahogany.

Considering she's close enough that we're practically touching, I suppose I can't ignore her any longer. I throw her a small smile and attempt to lighten the mood.

"Kaia, you could've told me you hated my shirt.

You didn't have to waste a drink."

She blushes under her freckles, and I swear it's the most beautiful thing I've ever seen.

"Oh my gosh, I'm so sorry!" She blushes again. "I wasn't paying attention, and I didn't see you."

She's flustered, which makes me feel slightly guilty for the cheeky line.

She reaches around the corner and grabs a stack of napkins from the holder at the end of the bar. She reaches up to pat my chest and seems to second guess herself, so she ends up sort of holding them between us.

"It's no problem, really."

I take the napkins and, in the process, brush her hand with mine. Electricity zips up my arm, and I know I should walk away now.

"Are you having a good time?" My mouth rebels against my sensibly-natured brain.

She smiles sheepishly. "I am, actually. I mean, I was. Until I ruined your ugly shirt."

I throw my head back and laugh. A genuine laugh, too. *Funny and beautiful.* A deadly combination...for me.

"I brought more than one shirt to Paris, Kaia, so

we're alright."

"Oi, mate—where have you been?" Lachlan stumbles up behind Kaia with two more shots in his hand, extending one in my direction.

We both take a half step back.

He hands me the shot and lifts the second with one arm, the other arm going around Kaia's shoulders. Whether that's out of affection or to keep himself from falling over, I'm not so sure. But if I had to put money on it? I'd say the latter.

Lachlan leans toward Kaia and, to her credit, she doesn't shy away from his breath, though I'm sure it smells like the bottom of a bottle. "Kaia, you know that you're the most beautiful woman in this pub, don't ya?"

I down the shot he handed me, if only for a reason to avert my eyes, and suppress a gag that threatens to make its way out of me, both at the comment and the liquor.

Raspberry vodka. *Really, Lachlan?*

Shaking my head quickly to erase the taste of it, I gesture toward our table and the rest of the group.

"Shall we?"

As Lachlan heads back to the booth with Kaia

under his arm, something settles in my stomach that hasn't been there in a long time. Something I'm going to have to ignore.

CHAPTER 7: KAIA

Imagine getting hit by a semi-truck…while having food poisoning. That about sums up how I feel this morning.

I press the heels of my hands into my eyes, trying to soothe away the headache pounding through every inch of my skull. I roll away from the sunlight peeking through the window, check the time on my phone, and groan. I drop it back onto the nightstand with a *thunk*. I am obviously not twenty-one anymore.

We have an excursion planned this morning, and every part of me wants to cancel and sleep the day away. But I didn't come all the way to Paris to sleep, as tempting as it sounds right now. I steel myself and sit up in bed, groaning the whole way. I immediately regret my decision as the onset of severe nausea creeps up my throat and the room spins like I'm on the scrambler at the county fair.

"Oh, God."

I throw my hand over my mouth, fighting with the covers to get my feet out of bed and onto solid ground, and run as fast as I can without falling over to the bathroom.

I'll spare you the details of what happened next, but I'm sure the sounds resembled that of an exorcism. On the bright side, I do feel a little more human now.

I soak a towel with cold water and hold it over my face, breathing in deeply, waiting for my body to settle before I reach for my toothbrush and delicately brush my teeth.

What on earth were we thinking getting so wild last night?

I take a couple of aspirin and slowly make my way back to my room. Then I open up the dresser drawers. Yes, I'm that person that unpacks on their trips. There's barely a closet, so anything that needs hanging is hung in the bathroom and on the curtain rods. I sift through my choices, and throw on my favorite vintage Levi's and a white crochet top, hoping I look a lot more put together than I feel. The finishing touch is running a brush through my hair.

I'm counting that as a win for the day.

I can hear the girls slowly making their way out of bed—a cacophony of collective groans and feet heavy on the floor as someone runs to the bathroom, highlighting how awful we're all feeling after last night.

It was a great night though, I think with a small smile as I attempt to wake my face up with mascara and concealer. *And we made some friends.*

I repeat *friends,* as if to reiterate to my brain that I'm not remotely interested in anything but friendship with anyone we met last night.

We all got along really well and ended up spending the whole night laughing, dancing, and drinking. Oh, so much drinking—which is why we all look like extras from *The Walking Dead* this morning.

"What time is our reservation?" Adelina yells from the other room.

"Stop yelling," Havannah groans.

I check the email confirmation. "We need to be

there in one hour!"

Several groans of discomfort come from the kitchen, where it sounds like someone is attempting to make coffee, thank God. Their groans describe my feelings exactly. And to think I didn't even want to go out last night. I could've avoided all of this. We all could have.

"We can do this. C'est la vie!"

"C'est la vie," Callie responds half-heartedly as she walks into my room. Judging by the dark smudges under her eyes, it looks like she didn't get a chance to take her makeup off last night. It took all we had just to make sure we made it back home and into bed, so I don't blame her.

I laugh. "Come on. That's all the enthusiasm you've got?"

"There's no coffee filters," she responds, fairly explaining her lackluster response.

"I'll run to the cafe down the street to grab some coffee and croissants. We'll put on some Mike Posner and have the best day ever!" I say as I loop my arm through hers and walk into the living room.

Havannah, who is laying on the couch with a pillow over her face, starts slow-clapping until Callie and Lina join in on this embarrassing but hilarious applause.

"Okay, I'm leaving," I say with a bow. "Be right back—with sustenance!"

I return with four coffees and a paper bag filled to the brim with croissants, two baguettes, and two kinds of jam. I smirk at the memory of the cafe worker after I put in my order.

"It's for me and my friends," I told him, but he continued to stare at me in disbelief, as if no one had ever ordered this much bread and coffee before.

"Oh, thank god!" Callie groans as she runs up to grab a coffee and croissant. "You're the best," she says through mouthfuls of flaky, buttery bread.

"I know." I wink. "How lucky you are to have a friend like me?"

We laugh as we devour our croissants and coffee as if our lives depend on it…and they kind of do.

I look down at my phone, and I'm reminded of the text message that lit up my phone at the crack of dawn this morning. It was from Lachlan, in a group chat, asking if we all wanted to grab dinner this week. How he was up so early, I'll never know, because I'm barely alive as it is. And he consumed far more alcohol than any of us…combined.

Havannah had responded, *Yes!* while I was out getting coffee and I'm not going to lie, I *am* looking forward to seeing them again. Some of them more than others, but I'm not willing to elaborate on that at the moment.

Adelina shuffles her feet toward me to grab a coffee and a croissant. She barely opens her eyes, avoiding the sunlight streaming in through the floor to ceiling windows in the provincial-style living room. Only enough to know she's not going to run into anything on the way over. At least she's dressed, and if I know Lina, I know she'll get through half of her coffee and be ready to rally.

Nursing our raging hangovers with coffee, croissants, and aspirin, we finish getting ready for the day. We're determined to make the most of our time here in Paris. Today we booked a scenic bike tour through the city with a local guide, and we're not going to miss it, no matter what mischief we may have gotten into last night.

We gather our courage, enough water to last us probably a week, a barf bag, and set out to meet our tour guide downstairs.

"If I die, Kaia gets my Chanel. I know she'll take care of it." Adelina straightens her sunglasses and clutches her stomach as if she might be sick.

"Ooh, the green one?" I jokingly squeal in excitement. "I mean, you better not croak. I need you!" I say as I hug her.

"I needed that hug," she says. "But also, if you do that again, I'm confident I will throw up on you."

I laugh and pick up my bike, setting my water bottle in the small cup holder in the middle of the frame.

I haven't been on a bike since college, when my best friend at the time and I rented bikes in Austin and got lost in the middle of a Texas July, sweating, and peddling, feeling like every street was uphill. I can look back on it and laugh now, but the anxiety I felt at the time was real. We walked funny for the next two days, and I can only pray that today's experience is much more leisurely. And surely, we won't get lost with a local guide.

As the tour guide gave us some directions and expectations for the tour, I can't help but feel a little apprehensive.

But before I can let myself get too into my head about it, we are mounting our bikes.

When in Paris, right?

We set off, a little off balance but righting ourselves as we peddle quickly to gain momentum. We turn toward the city center, watching carefully for cars. Already, I feel lighter. I realize fresh air and movement might be exactly what we need today.

As we ride through the streets of Paris, taking in all the sights and sounds of the city, I almost can't believe that I am here with my favorite people. The gorgeous architecture, the flowers hanging over the cafe awnings, the vendors on the streets, cars rushing past us at what seemed like lightning speed—it was exhilarating and terrifying all at the same time.

Will I die on this bike tour? Maybe. But will I die having the time of my life? Yes.

We pedaled past the *Louvre*, riding around the pyramid in the center of the atrium. We pull our bikes to the side to take pictures, posing and being goofy, per usual. You can tell our tour guide has done this a million times because he is no novice at getting perfect shots of us. We ride along the Seine River, watching the sun get higher in the sky, leaving a sparkle on the water. Pro tip: don't record a video of the Seine while bike riding unless you want to go for a swim.

Up next is a stop at *Notre Dame*. The cathedral is stunning, even from the outside. As I stare at it, it's as if time is standing still. I'm dying to get inside and soak up the sacred energy of the space, but our tour guide is already mounting his bike again, ready to take us to the pinnacle of the tour: the Eiffel Tower. I exhale a slow breath and I toss my leg over to follow the group.

"Are you sure this is safe?" I ask the guide as we stand very near a four way intersection at the base of the Eiffel Tower.

"*Oui!*" he shouts over the traffic. "I will get you the *best* photo from right here. Stand on that line—right there! Closer!"

We follow his commands and try to contain our shock as he lies on his stomach, getting ready to take our photo from the street.

"Smile, girls! We're in *Paris!*" Lina shouts.

The biggest grin breaks across my face as wind sweeps a section of my hair into my eyes. I can't help but feel like this is *the* moment. One that can't be beat. One that I'll replay in my mind and tell my grandchildren about one day. This is *magic*.

I can't help but feel alive and invigorated as we explore the city on two wheels. Hangovers long forgotten, this day has been full of laughter and learning about *la ville de l'amour* from our amazing tour guide. We found out he's a transplant from the French countryside, but he's lived in Paris with his wife and kids for the last twelve years. He's full of interesting facts and anecdotes about Paris, plus a recommendation for a cheese shop I *immediately* save in my phone.

Not to mention, I think I'm watching him and Adelina fall in love. To quote the great philosopher and queen, Taylor Swift, the sparks are flying all over the place.

After our excursion, we grab a coffee at a local cafe for a short debrief with the tour guide. He suggested grabbing a beer, but it's only eleven a.m., not to mention the wild night we just had, so we convinced him a *cafe au lait* would be more our speed this morning. He gives us some extra tips and tricks for our time here, as well as some must-see spots. My

Google Maps is full of little red dots to refer back to and visit.

"Okay," Callie says as she drains her cup and places it back on the table. "That was one of the highlights of the whole trip."

"I would one-hundred-percent do that again!" Havannah agrees.

It was hard *not* to agree. I haven't had that much fun in a long, long time, and the reality of that hits me harder the more time I spend in this incredible city.

I keep asking myself, when is the last time I felt this alive? And the answer is often, I have no idea.

I take a final sip of my coffee and glance at my best friends, sitting around this tiny cafe table, sun kissed from today's excursion, and I am so grateful.

Grateful they pushed me to take this trip.

Grateful for the sunshine.

Grateful for the memories I already know we are making.

Just…grateful.

CHAPTER 8: KAIA

Leave it to Havannah to find a restaurant for dinner on Instagram. I don't know how she does it, but it's a skill we have all learned to appreciate over the many years of friendship.

"Did you know they serve wine in baby bottles?" she says to Angus as we walk down the street to the fondue restaurant.

Supposedly, this restaurant can be hard to get into because it's so small, and the experience is so unique. We were told we'd have to wait over an hour after putting our names down to be seated, but we heard it's worth it. In the meantime, we're walking the streets surrounding the restaurant. We're father from the city center out here, and it feels like a more authentic Paris.

I find myself dragging toward the back of the group, walking a little slower to take everything in.

Lachlan falls into step beside me.

"How're you liking Paris, Kaia?"

I laugh and exhale. "How do I even put that into a sentence? Amazing doesn't even begin to cover this place. I love it here."

"I'm sure meeting each other has something to do with that, am I right?" he jokes.

"Oh, of course," I agree, playing up the sarcasm to match his tone. "It wouldn't be remotely as fun without you three to tag along on our adventures!"

His arm brushes mine, and I'm not entirely sure it was an accident.

"How long are you here for?" I ask, trying to steer us toward a safer topic.

"Depends on what my company needs. My flat is a permanent lease because I come back and forth so often."

"Ugh, what a dream."

Imagine having a permanent place in this city.

"Me or the flat?" He winks.

This guy is the king of charm, isn't he?

"Lachlan, *you* are trouble." I roll my eyes and bump him with my shoulder.

We end up getting dessert before dinner, stopping at a gelato stand on the side of the road. The girls and Angus, order ahead of me in near perfect French—we've been practicing—and I ask for two scoops, because how do you get anything less?

Lachlan orders a single scoop of strawberry then moves swiftly past me to pay for my gelato. Jack orders nothing.

"Thanks Lachlan. You didn't have to do that," I say shyly.

I'm not used to this kind of attention, to be honest, and I'm not really sure how to handle it.

"Yeah, Lach, you didn't pay for mine," Angus whines.

Lachlan looks at Angus before taking a leap onto his back, telling him he'll pay for his dinner if Angus will carry him all the way back to the restaurant. Angus shakes him off, punching him in the arm, which knocks Lachlan to the side.

Jack, who's been quiet and solitary the whole time, appears seemingly out of nowhere.

"Oi, gents, save it for the pitch."

He puts an arm around each of their necks and moves them to the front of the group.

Lina loops one arm through mine and gives me a knowing look.

"What?"

"As if it isn't obvious. First the rose, now paying for your gelato? Come on. It has all the makings of a Parisian *romance*." She sighs dreamily.

I get it. Isn't it every girl's dream to travel to Paris and fall in love and live happily ever after? Lachlan definitely has qualities that fit the bill. He towers over us girls, even me at five-foot-nine. Throw in his tan, dark hair, and blue eyes, and you've got a deadly combination.

So why don't I feel anything more than flattered? I wonder to myself as we approach the restaurant.

We end up waiting closer to two hours, so by the time we step into the restaurant, I'm starving. It's a step down to get inside, and the dining area is small. I mean, to the point of being cramped. There are only two tables in the whole restaurant, and they extend from the front to the back, running the entire length of the room, and the only walkway is in between. It has me wondering how people get to the inside of the table.

That mystery is quickly solved as I'm guided onto an empty chair, standing on it in my heels, my knees shaking slightly. I reach out my hands for balance, and someone grabs my left hand. I look down, surprised to find Jack keeping me steady.

"Thanks," I breathe.

I step onto the table, yes, *onto the table*, and onto the bench on the other side before letting go of Jack's hand and sliding into my seat.

My face is red from the attention, though the attention isn't on me for long as Lachlan basically cartwheels over the table to sit by me, his broad smile stretching from ear to ear as he settles in.

"I reckon this is gonna be a fun dinner!" He claps his hands together in excitement, and the group next to us jumps a little in alarm. I make eye contact with one girl at the table and mouth "sorry" with a small smile.

Lachlan probably doesn't need me to apologize for him—this is just who he is, the life of the party everywhere we've been.

Once we're all settled, with Havannah on my left and Lachlan on my right, the other four across from us, I allow my gaze to sweep the restaurant. It's completely packed, which in reality, is only about forty people. The walls are a faded yellow wallpaper with black trim, and they're covered with what looks like graffiti. The lighting is dim but comfortable and beyond the hum of the conversations around me, I can smell the melted cheese one of the servers dropped off to the couple next to Havannah, making my stomach growl.

I shift my legs, kicking someone in the tight quarters and quickly looking up to apologize when I make eye contact with Jack.

I forget whatever apology I was about to utter…I forget my own name. Were his shoulders that broad last night when I spilled my drink on him?

I recall his arms in the olive green shirt and swallow, my throat bobbing slightly.

"Sorry," I mutter.

"No worries." He responds with a tight smile, looking back at his menu.

"You okay?" I lean over and ask him.

"Ya, just fine," he replies, matter-of-fact, shifting in his seat, sending his shirt rippling over the muscles in his shoulders.

"Okay, well…I know we don't know each other super well, but if you ever need to talk or vent about anything, I'm here."

I glance down at my menu to give him the space he so clearly desires, but before I can, I notice he's looking directly at me for the first time all night.

He gives me a soft smile. "Thanks, Kaia."

I exhale and quickly tune into the conversation with the girls so I don't internalize and silently overthink myself into an anxiety attack.

I relax as the dinner continues and turns out, they do indeed serve their wine in baby bottles.

I swear I've laughed more tonight than I have the past year. Even Jack has loosened up. It's hard not to when you're thirty years old drinking from a baby bottle. The most hilarious thing is seeing Angus drink from one. The bottle looks like it was made for ants in his giant hands.

Another *cheers* echoes over the table from the seemingly never-ending baby bottles full of wine that specifically keep ending up in front of Lachlan.

This guy can drink…and drink. He's the epitome of a party guy, but he holds it together pretty well. To be honest, if I didn't know how much he's had to drink tonight, I might not know he's drunk by the way he's acting. He's so chill. Well, as chill as Lachlan can be. And he's *very* charismatic. The server falls more and more in love with him every time she walks over.

However, Lachlan hasn't paid much attention, not that she's noticed. Her eyes light up every time she looks at Lachlan, begging him to notice her.

I glance over at Jack again, almost without realizing it. He's been cold tonight. And I feel weird thinking that, because I don't know him well enough to decide whether or not I think he's actually being cold…but he is.

The Jack I'm seeing tonight is a far cry from the Jack who joked about the drink I spilled on his shirt last night, and I wish I didn't care. *I shouldn't care.*

He's deep in conversation with Angus across the table, and I'm trying to listen to Callie talk about the texts she's been exchanging with Jules. It's adorable to watch her get all flustered over him, and once we vet him and make sure he's not a serial killer, mark my words, they're going to be inseparable. I smile at Callie and reach over to grab one of her hands.

"I'm excited for you, Cal. Look at you! In Paris for a few days, and you've already found your Parisian

Prince Charming."

Callie blushes. "I'm trying not to get too ahead of myself, but…" She squeals quietly and her eyes light up. "It doesn't feel real! I mean, it still isn't. We've only texted!"

"We'll do our FBI roundup tonight to make sure he checks out!" Havannah says with a sly smile.

Lina adds, "He better have good intentions, or he's got us to answer to."

Agnus leans over. "And us!" he adds with gusto.

We laugh, but I'm guessing he's serious.

"Aw, thanks, Angus!" Callie says, leaning onto his shoulder in a sort of side hug, and Agnus gestures with his hands, making it look like he's doing a curtsey.

Jack shifts in his seat, his knee brushing mine below the table, and my brain goes blank.

I no longer hear the noise of the restaurant. I'm only vaguely aware of Lachlan cracking a joke that has the rest of the group chuckling, but that point of contact with Jack is all I can think about. The warmth that spreads from my knee to deep in my stomach… and the fact that he doesn't immediately move, are seared into my brain.

There's no way this is in my head.

I swear he lingered for at least ten seconds before clearing his throat and moving his leg away. Not that I counted.

The loss is immediate, the warmth leaving me as quickly as it came. I'm thinking Jack feels it, too, because he glances at me but quickly looks away.

Lachlan's voice breaks through the moment like a brick slamming through a glass window. "Dessert round two, anyone?"

CHAPTER 9: JACK

I could kick myself for how I acted tonight, I think as I sink into the plush couch in the living room, my head sinking into my hands. I press my palms into my eyes until I see stars, trying to erase the memories of my awful attitude during what could have been, and should have been, a really great night.

It's been a work in progress, trying to force myself to have fun, to behave like a normal human would after the past few years I've had. It would be the understatement of the century to say I've had my guard up. My walls are so high that I barely looked in Kaia's direction all night. Not that it matters, and she probably didn't even notice, though she's all I seem to notice.

I press my hands harder into my eyes, until it almost hurts, but I can't seem to erase the memory of Kaia standing on that chair and holding my hand for balance. Her breathy voice as she thanked me echoes in my head, like it was meant for me and only me. We might as well have been the only two people in the restaurant.

I whisper a quiet prayer that something else, *anything else*, will occupy my mind for the rest of the trip. Because right now, it's inundated with all things Kaia.

My mind quickly flashes back to the pictures the girls were showing off at dinner of their bike tour that morning, and I'm picturing Kaia in a pair of distressed jeans with her arms raised, her shirt skimming just above her belly button, in front of *Notre Dame*, that perfect smile spread across her face.

My prayers are useless. They can't undo the fact that we've met and that devastatingly beautiful smile lives rent-free in my head.

That feels dramatic, but the truth is that she's practically all I've thought about since I saw her for the first time in that pub.

And last night, while I was busy being broody, she

was beyond cheerful, soaking up each moment, even taking time to check up on me when she noticed I didn't seem to be as into the festivities as the rest of the bunch.

Toward the end of the dinner, I not-so-accidentally brushed my knee against her leg, needing to be close to her, like she's a magnet I can't help but be drawn to.

And like a magnet, I stayed, touching her, feeling the pressure of her leg against mine. It was an idiotic move. I quickly realized how problematic it could be, and I shifted, immediately feeling the loss of her presence. I could be imagining things, but I think she felt the loss, too. Though I can't be sure, because I barely said two words to her all night, as if she'd done something to cause me great personal harm.

But it's not that at all. My bad mood started back at Lachlan's flat well before dinner. He's been talking about Kaia nearly nonstop since we met them at the pub, and to be quite frank, it's getting old.

It's not even that *he's* talking about her, it's more that I can't. I can't talk about the way her laugh warms my entire body, like my favorite cup of coffee. Or the way the dimple in her left cheek is highlighted when she's really excited about something. I can't talk about any of that, but Lachlan gets to. Because he called dibs. And I'm not ready to face all the things I think I could feel for her. I need to just leave it alone.

I think I need a few days to get over it. I mean, we've only just met, *and we're in the City of Love.* I roll my eyes even as I think it, but I'd be remiss to ignore the allure of romance in Paris. I'm sure these feelings will blow over soon, and I can focus on having normal, human interactions with her—where I don't feel like I have to avoid her to keep my emotions in check.

"Hey, mate—you good? You seemed pretty on edge at dinner." Angus walks into the living room after showering. We all headed straight home after dinner, eager for a night of doing nothing after a unexpectedly wild night at the pub.

"Oh, ya, all good. Just an off day," I say in my best attempt at nonchalance.

Angus plops himself on the couch, causing me to about go flying. Practically made of stone, that one. Built like a Greek statue, he probably weighs almost the same. He's the definition of someone who doesn't realize their own strength.

He chuckles and apologizes.

"You know, you don't have to pretend." He's not looking at me when he says it. Instead, he's opened up a book he brought with him. Another thing about Angus is he's a huge book nerd. He's got a floor-to-ceiling, wall-to-wall bookshelf completely packed with books in his apartment back home, and it's a masterpiece—a book lover's dream.

I steal a glance at him, appreciation for my friend turning the corner of my mouth up into a small smile. Would you believe me if I told you this gentle giant of a human is reading Jane Austen? He's a big ol' softie and has a heart for the classics.

"I don't know what you mean," I say, and it's partially true. I'm not confident I know what he's talking about, but I also know how perceptive and smart he is, so I'm thinking there's a slight chance whatever he's talking about has to do with the fact that I've been completely shutting down around Kaia.

"Whatever you're thinking about right now…the thing you're questioning whether or not I know?" he says, elbow on the armrest and hand under his chin, nose deep in *Emma*. It's a sight to see.

He finally looks over at me, making direct eye contact.

"I know."

I sigh and look away.

"I picked up on it right away in the pub, mate. You *like* her," he chuckles.

I hate how perceptive he is.

I roll my eyes and take a deep breath.

"Look, even if that was true…and I'm not saying it is, it doesn't matter."

"No?"

"No," I state very matter-of-fact, my emotions completely undetectable. "It doesn't matter because Lachlan's made his interest clear."

And I didn't come to Paris to date a girl I just met, especially after the last couple of years. I don't say that last part out loud because I know Angus will want to talk to me about it and ask how I'm doing.

I'm doing fine, for someone whose fiancé left him at the altar almost two years ago. Yep, that doesn't just happen in movies and bad reality TV shows. It happens in real life. Well, my life anyway.

Honestly, I probably should've seen it coming. I ignored every damn red flag leading up to the wedding because I was so head-over-heels, stupid in love with Evie.

We met at uni. She sat next to me in stats class, and I finally worked up the courage to pass her a cheeky note one day. It was game day, and she was on the basketball team, so she was wearing the team jersey. It was an ocean blue that brought out the blue in her eyes. A blue that sparkled with amusement as her eyes met mine after reading,

"Need a good luck charm at your game tonight?" I'd asked, *with the answers, "Yes or Yes,"* and instructions to circle one, signed with a wink face and my name.

Pretty smooth, I know.

I wish I could tell some grandiose story about her shooting a buzzer beating shot to win the game and finding me in the crowd afterward to confess her deep adoration for me. They actually lost the game, but I invited her out for a slice of pizza afterward—because pizza fixes everything—and the rest was history.

Was.

We dated for three years before I proposed. Then, we were engaged for two years before the wedding. I was ready for a shotgun wedding after I proposed. I couldn't *wait* to start our lives together. She didn't want to rush things, though. She told me we had all the time in the world and "the rest of our lives doesn't need to start right now." Whatever that means.

Red flag number one.

I zone back into reality and complete my thought to Angus. "So, the problem is solved. In fact, there's not even a problem to solve, mate. Everything is a-okay," I say, putting some extra drawl on the "a-okay."

He laughs out loud this time, closing his book. "Everything is not *a-okay*. Where'd you go just now?" Realization flashes across his face. "Oh. *Oh*. Evie. You wanna talk it out?"

He barely gets the last word out before I cut him off.

"No." I'm harsher than I intend to be, but I'm not currently seeking advice from my emotionally stable friend who has a happy, healthy relationship with his girlfriend of over two years.

"No, thank you," I continue. "There's nothing to talk about."

The woman I thought I'd spend the rest of my life with ended our relationship the same way it started:

with a note. This one said she was "sorry" and that she "tried," my mom's engagement ring tucked inside like it meant nothi—

I stop my train of thoughts before they derail. A vacation to Paris isn't the time to stew about how devastating my last break up was. I sit up straight and move my head from side to side, cracking my neck. I look over at Angus, who's been quiet, as if he's been waiting for me to speak. Sympathy is written all over his face. It quickly shifts to understanding and acceptance when I give him a look, telling him not to push me right now. The understanding that I would very much like to change the subject.

He looks down at his book with a sad smile.

"You're right, mate. Everything's a-okay. But if for some reason, it's ever *not* a-okay, I'll be here to pick up the pieces when, I mean…*if* you idiots need me to."

"Who are you calling idiots?" Lachlan yells, his booming voice for sure echoing into the apartments next to us.

He walks into the living room from his designated office. He had been in there sending emails and putting out fires at work like the big boss man he is. He developed an app called The QuestFriends Guild a few years back that helps you find people with similar interests to go on specific adventures and excursions with you in various cities. It's actually pretty cool, and I'm really proud of him.

"Well, well, well. Look who graced us with his presence!" I say, acting impressed by his entrance.

Our love language for each other is sarcasm, so if at any point you're worried we don't like each other, don't be. This is how we say "I love you," because we're too emotionally damaged to admit aloud how we actually feel and too proud to go to therapy to unlearn it.

"It was the legal team. Apparently, there's a competing app out there trying to copy our operational model. Regardless—cease and desist is delivered. All good, mates."

Lachlan plops down on a comfy chair in the corner of his living room. He looks exhausted. To his credit, Lachlan works extremely hard. Probably harder than he should, but he cares about his company and the people who work for him. He's one of the best examples of a boss that I've ever witnessed. But I also think he gives too much of himself to his work, always trying to think of the next big thing or plan a huge event, and it's clear he's burned out. He chalks it up to working hard and playing harder. Which I guess is accurate for him, because he does *work* hard, but he *parties* harder than anyone I've ever met. He's essentially a professional partier. Around here, chances are if someone is hosting a party, they've heard of Lachlan and want him there.

"Are we playing Diablo tonight, or what?" Lachlan asks, eyes closed and head leaning back like he's about to fall asleep.

"Can't. Got a date with Jane." Oh, Angus.

"Mate, you look like you're about the pass out right there. Why don't you go to bed?" I say.

"Yeah, yeah, Mum. Five more minutes of playtime, and then I'll go to bed."

Lachlan gets up, as if determined to prove he's always got it in him for fun. He throws me a controller, and he and I get ready to play.

It seems we're both pretending our problems don't exist tonight.

CHAPTER 10: KAIA

We've spent practically every day with the guys since we met them at the pub. If you would have told me that our girls trip would have turned into a combined trip with a group of handsome guys from Australia, I would've canceled my flight and stayed home, but I am honestly so glad I didn't.

I can't seem to explain the instantaneous connection that we've all got, but I often find myself forgetting I haven't known these guys my entire life. If it weren't for the difference in our accents, I'm guessing we could fool everyone into thinking we all traveled here together from the same place.

Lachlan lives here, so while he indulges us girls with our need to participate in all of the touristy things Paris has to offer, he's also got a good handle on living like a local, due to his company's presence in Europe. He's clued us in to some of the *best* kept secrets Paris has to offer.

Earlier in the week, we ventured over to *Sacre-Coeur*, a stunning Basilica perched high on a hill on the outskirts of Paris.. Little did we know when we planned the day, we'd spend a solid twenty minutes climbing a seemingly never ending spiral staircase up to the top. The staircase was barely wide enough for one person, going either way, and the ceiling wasn't quite tall enough for most of us to stand up fully. Havannah, at only five-foot-three was just fine. We climbed the whole way, slightly hunched over, and it took all of five minutes to inspire Callie and I to do our best *Hunchback of Notre Dame*—or should I say, Hunchback of *Sacre-Coeur*—impersonation almost the rest of the way up. We hunched our shoulders and sang songs from the film, the words echoing off the stone walls.

We probably added an extra five minutes to our climb because we all had to stop and catch our breath, both from said climb and how hard we were laughing at each other.

Once we finally got to the top, though, you didn't hear a sound out of any of us for at least thirty seconds. The view of the city from the top of *Sacre-Coeur* literally leaves you speechless. Words wouldn't do it justice.

"Holy shit," Lachlan whispers.

Yeah, not even those words.

I wander to an overlook and lean out, letting my hair blow in the breeze. It's a little foggy today, but fog can't mask the beauty of this city. I exhale and close my eyes. Someone moves next to me, and I figure one of the girls came to join me.

I open my eyes to see Lachlan's dark hair ruffling in the wind, his eyes closed. He's rarely quiet, but right now, he looks downright contemplative.

He opens his eyes and smiles at me, and I look away quickly, my cheeks flushed.

"Enjoying the view?" he asks.

For a second, I feel the need to roll my eyes, but I realize Lachlan isn't trying to feed me a line; he's genuinely curious about my experience.

I return his smile and nod.

For a minute or two, we soak it all in. He slides a little closer to me, and I turn to face him, instinctively taking a half step back.

"I'm really glad I met you," he says.

"Me too," I tell him genuinely.

He closes in another half step.

"All of us meeting has been the best thing to happen on this trip!" I try to diffuse the situation by talking about us in a group setting. "Let's get a group shot up here! Girls! Get over here!"

Safe and sound in our group, I settle in between Lina and Callie, Havannah on Lina's other side, and the boys gather behind us, the stunning view of Paris behind them.

Angus uses his height and long arms to stretch out and capture our first, *but not our last*, group shot, selfie-style.

No one decides to play hunchback on the way down, and I'm not sure whether that's due to the subdued experience of the view and Basilica, or because we all need to catch our breath this time. We're making our way down the spiral staircase, and I'm trying to contain my breathing so it's not obvious that I'm fighting for my life here.

With the rest of the group ahead of me, I pause for a minute to catch my breath and compose myself.

I can barely hear the rest of the group now.

Wow, they got ahead fast.

I make my way to resume the spiral staircase of death, but instead, something, or rather someone, runs into the back of me, making my heart jump in my throat.

The two strong hands on either of my shoulders are the only reason I didn't fall face forward down the stairs.

I turn around to see who gave me this near-death experience, and my brown eyes meet green as I look up into Jack's face.

"Kaia, I'm so sorry!" he exclaims. "I ran up to get a couple more shots with the fog lifted and was looking at my phone on the way down. I didn't see you."

I let out a breath and smile up at him. "It's okay, really. I'm surprised I haven't managed to accidentally fling myself down these stairs anyway. I'm usually pretty clumsy."

I shrug my shoulders to emphasize it's no big deal, and realize his hands are still on me. He quickly drops them, as if he realizes that same thing.

"Oh, sorry," he says gruffly.

I take a step up toward him. "No, I didn't mean —"

He takes a step down as I take my step up. When we realize we are both headed in the same direction, we sort of sidestep, in that awkward way when you don't know which direction someone is going. I press my back into the wall of the staircase, and I swear this staircase got even smaller with my proximity to Jack. He turns to move past me, his back against the opposite wall, causing him to hunch over a bit.

Our chests are practically touching, and his face is inches from mine.

If I thought I needed to catch my breath before, that's no problem now. I forgot how to breathe at this point.

His shoulders are so broad he takes up most of the space, and I find myself pushing further back into the stone. His chest is moving rapidly, though he isn't making any sound. I force myself to take a breath before I pass out.

I inhale slowly, attempting to steel my nerves, which appeared out of nowhere.

He smells like pine, a comforting, familiar scent, the kind that feels like home.

I exhale slightly and look up into his eyes. We haven't been this close since I spilled my drink on him in the pub.

"Um," I say, breaking the silence.

"Right." He nods quickly.

"I'll just—" I shift my body in an attempt to move down the stairs. Jack moves at the same time, and we bump heads.

Each holding our own forehead, we make eye contact once more and let out an awkward laugh, diffusing…whatever tension had settled over us.

"Kaia, I promise I am not trying to kill you on this staircase," he chuckles softly.

"You could've fooled me," I joke.

He flashes me a broad smile, and laugh lines around the edge of his mouth appear.

I wonder what it takes to make him laugh hard enough to earn those lines.

As if he can read my mind, he tenses slightly and his smile fades. "We should catch up, yeah?"

I look toward the bottom of the staircase.

"Oh, yeah, absolutely!"

He gestures with his arm. "After you."

"Oh, a gentleman. *Merci, monsieur.*" I think about

dipping into a curtsey, but I've had too many close calls on these stairs as it is, so instead I step down and face forward, being very careful with my steps as I start the rest of the trek down.

Jack says nothing the rest of the way, his silence ringing in my ears.

I step into the sunshine to find the rest of the group waiting, and Jack steps out a few moments later as if he intentionally put space between us.

Lina looks at me curiously, but I only shrug. I'm starving and don't have the brain power to think about how being so close to Jack made me feel like my heart was going to beat straight out of my chest.

Almost on cue, Lachlan claps his hands together, and says, "Where to next, gang?"

I'm convinced he only has two volumes when he speaks—either so quiet you have no idea what he's saying, or it's loud as hell.

Before anyone can answer, he turns to me and reaches out to brush my elbow with his hand. "Where would you like to go next, Kai?" He smiles at me, and I appreciate the gesture, but I also feel a little strange to be the only one to suggest where we go next. I have too much anxiety about whether or not everyone else is having fun to do that.

"I'm totally down to do what everyone else wants to do!" I say, probably too enthusiastically.

I'm too tired, and honestly, a little *too* relaxed to care.

Too relaxed? Who is she?

Adelina meets my eye with a knowing look on her face. "Let's go hang at a coffee shop for a bit."

And this is why we're besties. She knew that's exactly what I wanted to do, but I'm too worried about everyone being happy to risk picking the wrong activity.

The group agrees, and we start walking in the direction of a nearby cafe that's apparently famous for its chocolate cake.

Lachlan comes up beside me and throws his bent arm out, gesturing for me to loop mine through. I look up at him, and he winks. A wink that I'm sure makes girls weak in the knees when it's coupled with that million-dollar smile.

"Can't have you tripping on these cobblestones, mate."

He must've seen me stumble as we were walking out of *Sacre-Coeur.* I was hoping no one saw that.

I loop my arm through his and resume walking, and once again attempt to deny the reality that is Lachlan's flirty disposition.

He's just being friendly, I think to myself.

And he isn't the handsome Australian I want to be flirting with, my heart seems to whisper in response.

I glance over at Jack instinctively, and find him looking at the ground as he walks, hands deep in his pockets, his face tense.

CHAPTER 11: KAIA

Today, we decide to go to a farmers market to pick up some ingredients to make lasagna, a summer salad, and garlic bread, and have the guys over for dinner. It felt like the perfect I'm-pretending-to-be-local-to-Paris type of day. Lachlan technically does live here, so I guess not all of us are pretending.

It's great having Lachlan with us because, not only does he know all the fun spots not overwhelmed by tourists, but he also seems to know *everyone*. It's as if he says hi to someone he knows everywhere we go.

I guess I can't be too surprised. He *is* the guy in the room that everyone is drawn to. He has a magnetic personality, and it's interesting watching people move toward his sphere of existence, almost like they can't help themselves. I mean, he is sort of the reason we're all even together right now, so I can understand the pull.

While wandering the farmer's market, I can't help but pretend that this is my real, everyday life. I know it's real in the sense that I am here, in Paris, with a bag full of tomatoes and basil, a baguette hanging out of the top, but I've never been this relaxed, this at peace. And I get it: I'm on a *dream* vacation with my very best friends, but when I think about returning to real life in two short weeks, my heart races with anxiety, and I'm overwhelmed with dread. Take the Sunday scaries and multiply it by ten. That's what it feels like when I think about going home after this trip. I didn't expect to feel this way. In fact, I expected the opposite.

Something about my face must be off, because Lina comes over from a tent where she was smelling different homemade soaps with Angus.

"What's the matter? Do you need more Euros?"

I look down at the fresh mozzarella I'm holding.

"Oh, no," I laugh. "I just…I never want this to end."

I look up and give her a small smile.

"I wish this was our normal, everyday life," I tell her truthfully.

"I get it," she responds, handing the vendor a few bills for the cheese, looping her arm through mine and turning me toward a row of buckets filled with fresh flowers. "This *is* the dream. Wandering the farmers market, no work to worry about, no mean boss to yell at you…"

I give her a pointed look. Lina is a freelance illustrator, so she can work from anywhere in the world. I've caught her on her laptop quite a bit, and I even think I heard her once around three a.m. on the phone with a client.

"Okay, *some* work," she concedes. "But Kai, I love what I do. It's not like I'm working until nine p.m. for an asshole who doesn't even know my name."

Oof. She got me there.

"Point taken."

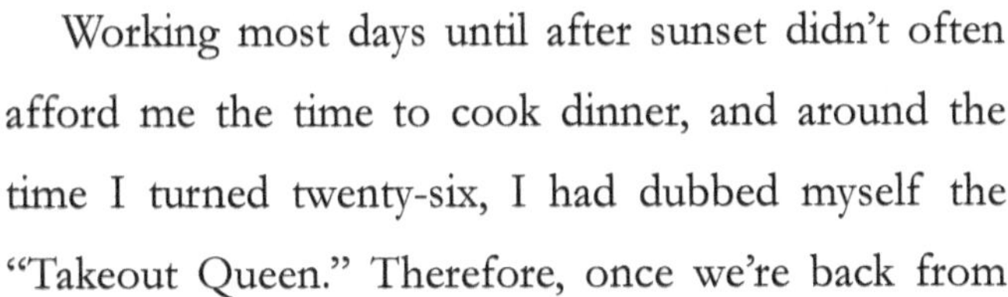

Working most days until after sunset didn't often afford me the time to cook dinner, and around the time I turned twenty-six, I had dubbed myself the "Takeout Queen." Therefore, once we're back from the market, I park myself on one of the mismatched chairs at the kitchen table. This table is stunning—made of solid wood and set in a natural stain. I bet this table could tell so many stories about the people who've sat around it and broke bread.

I pour myself a glass of champagne.

"What're we celebrating?" Agnus asks.

A look at my confused face has him motioning toward the green bottle on the table.

"Angus," I say seriously, "champagne *is* the celebration."

He laughs, and I lift my glass in a mock toast before taking another sip.

Jack and Callie are at the counter in the kitchen, doing all of the prep work for our meal. I can't help but notice Jack in an apron, simple gray and white, tied around his waist. I smile at the sight and turn to see Havannah, sitting on one of the other countertops, in conversation with Lachlan. Lina is nowhere to be seen.

I'm about to get up and look for her when I notice her iPad is missing from the table, where it's been almost the entire trip. I look around further and see her through the window, sitting on a chair outside, drawing.

"She's an artist, huh?" Angus asks me.

"She's incredible. She's been trying to finish this book cover for a fantasy novel, so I'm sure that's what she's out there working on."

"A book cover?" Angus sounds more than intrigued.

"Oh, go on, Angus."

I hadn't noticed that Lachlan had wandered over to us until he spoke.

"Angus would live in a library if he could," Lachlan explains.

As if he needed to prove Lachlan's statement true, Agnus excuses himself to go outside and chat with Lina about this book. Lachlan, however, pulls out a chair, turns it around, and tosses a leg over the side before leaning his chin on the back.

"Hi," he says casually.

"Hi," I reply in my best attempt at casual.

I mean, I want to be casual. But the way he's looking at me is…whatever the opposite of casual is. I take another sip of my champagne so I have something to do with my hands.

"So I take it I shouldn't call you Chef Kaia?" he

smirks.

"How ever did you figure that out?" I ask sarcastically.

"You didn't even try to help—just sat right down with your champagne."

"Oh, I know better than to be in the way of Callie in the kitchen." I jerk my chin toward the woman in question.

Callie and Jack are busy washing produce, slicing bread, steaming and peeling the tomatoes, and trying to keep Havannah from eating all of the cheese. Seeing them in the kitchen together is like seeing a choreographed dance. In the same way that I don't love to cook, Callie is meant to be in the kitchen. And from the looks of it, Jack is, too.

I've yet to see him this relaxed. For once, his shoulders are away from his ears, and he's been wearing a small smile nearly the entire time he's been in there. Not that I've been *looking* at him the entire time he's been in there. I look back at Lachlan, who was looking at me, looking at Jack.

I give him a small smile and take another sip of champagne.

"Want some?" I ask.

"I'm already set," he holds up a beer, cheersing my glass. "To you, Kaia. I've been in Paris an awful lot, but it's never quite captured my attention as it has on this trip."

I flush. "Well, that's sweet," I say quietly, hoping no one else heard his words.

He moves his chair a little closer to the table, grabbing the bottle and pouring me a little more.

When did my class get empty?

"So what's your favorite part of your trip so far? I know you still have some time here."

I consider my answer. This trip has been incredible, every part special in its own way. There have been so many unique memories made that it's hard to narrow down a top moment.

"Hmm." I take another sip. "I'd say getting to see Paris in a way that locals do. We saw so much on our bike tour that we wouldn't have gotten to otherwise. Plus, you've been the most helpful guide for the best cafes and secret spots!"

"I aim to please," Lachlan says with a beaming smile.

I turn slightly, aiming to shift the conversation away from me.

"Havannah, what's been your favorite part?"

"Easy," she says, sliding off the counter and grabbing her wine glass, which is filled with a true, French red. "The bread."

"The bread," Callie practically moans from the kitchen.

We all laugh, but I have to agree: the French don't mess around with their bread and their cheese. Lina and Angus walk back inside as we attempt to compose ourselves.

"What's so funny?" Angus asks.

"Callie is having romantic feelings about French bread," Havannah jokes.

"Aren't we all," Lina responds with a wink.

"I know I am," Angus adds, patting his stomach. "When's dinner?"

"We just put the lasagna in. It'll be about fifteen minutes," Jack says, wiping his hands on a towel.

"What are we going to do for fifteen minutes?" Angus asks with a bit of a whine.

"Drinking game!" Lachlan suggests with gusto.

"No." The response came from Angus and Jack simultaneously, causing Lachlan to groan and us girls to laugh.

"We can talk about our plan for tomorrow?" Callie, our planner extraordinaire, suggests while tossing the salad. "We're going to the *Louvre* in the morning, and have reservations for dinner, but could use some suggestions for lunch!"

"The *Louvre*!" Angus looks the same way he did when he found out Lina was illustrating a book cover.

"You haven't been yet?" I ask him.

"I haven't! Mind if I tag along?"

"We all will!" Lachlan exclaims. Not that we mind, but it's such a Lachlan thing to do. "That way I can show you the best cafe in the area after. Plus, there's a vendor over there who sells art prints that I think you would be really interested in, Adelina."

That is also such a Lachlan thing to do. He may give me a little extra attention, but he really does care that everyone in our group has the best time.

"It's a date!" I say, obviously not thinking about my words, and I regret them immediately. Jack looks up from slicing the bread, and Lachlan smiles knowingly.

"Kaia, want to help me set the table?" Lina asks, once again coming to my rescue.

And just like that, the moment is diffused.

The table is set with mismatched, but color-coordinated floral plates and an array of wine glasses, champagne glasses, and beer bottles. Steam rises from the lasagna at the center, offering an enticing aroma to us as we all take our seats. Jack starts to serve the summer salad that's been prepared. He reaches across the table to put a serving on my plate, and we make eye contact. I'm vaguely aware of the rest of the table continuing in conversation, of Jack slowly releasing the spoons so the mix of lettuce, strawberries, and feta fall on my plate, but I'm unable to focus on anything but his eyes.

Green, not like grass or emeralds, but softer, more muted. Like the underside of a leaf in the shade. And they are looking at me with such a wistful expression.

While our eye contact seemed to last an hour, it had to have been no more than five or ten seconds before he moved on to continue dishing out the salad. I sit further back in my seat, trying to focus on dinner, on my best friends and new friends sharing this meal together, and not on whatever that expression in Jack's eyes must have meant.

Before bed, the girls and I chat over the last two bottles of red at our Airbnb, and I make a mental note to pick up some more tomorrow. After our delicious lasagna dinner, we opted to drink right from the bottle to avoid dirtying more dishes that took way too long to wash. *Does anyone in France own a dishwasher?*

I know we're only drinking wine together in a living room like any other girl's night, but this is a highlight of the trip. This is the reason I'm here: to spend time with my best friends. Right as I'm about to get deep in my feelings, Callie switches topics.

"Okay, okay," she giggles. That's the number one clue that Callie's been drinking: she's got the giggles. "Off the record—who would you date out of the three of them, you know, if you had to?" Callie looks toward Adelina, raising the wine bottle to her lips, smiling as she waits for her answer.

Havannah and I lean closer to Adelina, and I'm desperate to not miss one syllable of this vital piece of information. This is what I imagine finding a treasure map on the back of the Declaration of

Independence feels like.

Or maybe that's the wine talking.

"You guys are ridiculous, you know that?" She rolls her eyes. "I would *never*"—she pauses to look at us to really nail her point home— "Never. But, if I *had* to…"

Please don't say Jack. The thought tugs at the corner of my mind, and I'll continue to pretend as though thoughts like that don't exist, thank you very much.

"Angus!" Lina immediately covers her face with her hands and squeals.

Callie jumps slightly, tucking her knees under her before returning to her spot on the couch. She juts the wine bottle in Lina's direction.

"I knew it!" Callie yells.

Adelina rolls her eyes as she grabs the bottle from Callie's hand and takes a sip.

"Okay, what about you, Cal?"

"Oh, that's easy. Jules!"

"That doesn't count!" Havannah whines. "He wasn't part of the game!"

"Well, who would you pick?"

Havannah considers this.

"I mean, physically? Angus!"

No one of us are actually surprised by this. Havannah typically dates guys who are almost a foot taller than her.

"But…" Lina pressures.

"I guess Lachlan!"

"Really?" I can't keep the surprise out of my voice.

The girls look at me knowingly.

"What?" I ask, grabbing the wine bottle from Lina.

"Genuinely curious, Kai," Callie starts suggestively. "Who would you pick?"

I swear, it has never been this quiet at a girls' night before, everyone is looking at me expectantly and I know they're not going to let me out of this without answering.

"Angus, obviously!" I say, my voice serious and steady.

It's silent for another few beats, and I take another drink from the bottle.

All of the sudden Callie bursts out laughing, Adelina and Havannah losing it shortly after.

As we sit together, crowded on this couch in Paris, happiness settles deep within my bones. Paris is my favorite place in the whole world, and these friends are my favorite people.

CHAPTER 12: KAIA

We're at the *Louvre* today.

The Louvre.

In Paris.

I am still not over it. We've been here for about thirty minutes, and I'm already blown away by the beauty of this place, and the magnitude of incredible art housed here. I'm almost scared to walk through these halls, afraid of accidentally breaking something.

Do I even own enough money to be looking at this art? I jokingly think to myself.

I'm looking at the *Winged Victory of Samothrace*, you know, the one in that Beyonce video, when someone walks up next to me. I turn to find Jack. My heart begins racing, and something akin to electricity runs down my arms, making my hair stand up slightly.

Why am I so nervous?

"Hey, Jack!" I say, over-enthusiastically.

I cringe. I'm trying to hide my nervousness, but I'm clearly overcompensating.

He chuckles and runs a hand over the back of his neck, locking eyes with me as he looks up. His shirt stretches over the muscles in his arm and chest as his hand pulls on the hem that's ridden up just enough for me to catch a glimpse of the tan skin underneath.

I immediately look back at the sculpture.

"Hey, Kaia. Enjoying yourself?"

"Oh, so much!"

Gosh, I'm being so weird.

Chill out, Kaia.

I force myself to take a slow, deep breath, exhaling through my nose and praying it's not noticeable. I turn to face him, feigning confidence.

"Are you enjoying *your*self?" I ask.

He looks away from the art, and his eyes find mine. If he couldn't hear my heart pounding before, I'm absolutely sure he can now. I'm sure I'm staring, but I legitimately cannot help it. He's so handsome. I had already noticed and recalled only eight hundred times, the exact shade of green his eyes are, but standing this close I can see specks of gold hidden among the leafy green, perfectly complementing the golden tones of his artfully messy hair, which I'm definitely not thinking about running my fingers through.

Good God, he belongs here in this museum with the rest of the art.

I break free from the spell to return my attention to the artwork in front of us.

"I am now," he says, and because Jack is often so careful with his words, I can't help but ponder the meaning of them.

I look up at him and smirk.

"Oh, yeah? It's this sculpture, isn't it?" I nod my head toward the piece.

"Ah, yes. You guessed it. I have been eyeing her since we got here." He chuckles and gives a jokingly bashful smile.

"Well, I mean, don't let me interrupt this *monumental* moment. Now's your chance to tell her how you feel," I say, gesturing to the statue in front of us, but a flash of concern or concentration spreads across Jack's face as he looks at me and then back to the piece of art.

It's there and gone so quickly it's impossible to know what it was, especially now that it's been replaced by a crooked smile.

"You sure it's not too late? I imagine she's had many suitors vying for her hand at this point. I don't suppose she'd go for a bloke like me, do ya?"

The air feels like it's been sucked out of the room, and I'm suddenly not sure we're talking about the statue anymore. Jack is staring at me now, a half smile on his face, some unreadable emotion in his eyes. I wish more than anything that I could get inside that head of his.

"I think…" I pause, contemplating my answer. "I think she'd be lucky to have a *bloke* like you," I say, nudging his arm with my shoulder.

Who am I?

We're sorry, Kaia can't come to the phone right now. She's dead, and her ballsy alter-ego has taken over.

Jack throws his hand over his heart, his face shining with pride, as though he's the most honored he's ever been by the compliment. After a moment of fake seriousness, we both break into a laugh.

"That's high praise, mate," he says, and once again, I can feel his eyes on me. I don't dare look away from the sculpture. I don't dare face whatever emotion shines in those green eyes.

I study the sculpture for every extra second I can manage to avoid eye contact. "Don't get used to it, Thompson," I say, trying to be serious and realizing this might be the first time I've ever said his last name out loud. "I like your head the exact size it is, so I don't want to inflate it too much."

Jack throws that perfect head of his back and laughs, and I want to replay the sound over and over again. This time, when his gaze locks on mine, I don't turn away. I let myself lock eyes with him, holding my breath.

Is it me, or are we suddenly much closer than we were a moment ago?

"Kaia, I—" Jack starts, moving to close the small gap between us, but he's interrupted when the rest of the group finds us.

"Hey, friend! We've been looking all over for you," Adelina says. "Isn't this the one in the Beyonce video?"

See?

Jack and I share a quick look before walking over to join the group, putting much more distance between us than is probably necessary. I shove away all thoughts over that interaction that attempt to flood my brain.

Could I be reading things wrong? There's no way that wasn't flirting, right?

I try not to think too much about that moment as we wander through the remainder of the museum, and with some of the world's most incredible art on display, it's easy to be distracted. I remind myself I didn't come to Paris with the plan to find romance…I didn't come to Paris with much of a plan at all, which is so unlike me.

Am I simply discovering more about who I am outside of a twelve-by-twelve office in a high rise? Maybe Kaia in Paris *is* flirty and interested in romance. Maybe my new lack of a ten-year plan is leaving room for me to be more adventurous. Or maybe, I'm feeling inspired by the art.

Yeah, it's probably the art.

After walking endlessly through the museum—and

getting lost a few times myself—we're all starving. Angus chooses our dinner place this time: an Indian restaurant that serves the best naan in all of Europe —according to the owner, that is. And while I haven't tasted every kind of naan in Europe to confirm, I can confirm it was pretty dang amazing.

Jack and I end up at opposite ends of the table. Whether or not that was intentional isn't important, nor is it a thought I'm currently giving any weight to…or at least trying not to.

Almost out of habit, I find myself glancing to his end of the table. I seem to do that instinctually every time I think about him, which has been a lot lately. When I look over at him, I see him already looking at me. He gives me a soft smile before returning his attention to his menu, and my stomach seems to have become occupied by a bunch of rather large butterflies.

"How's the trip so far, Kai?" My reverie is broken as Lachlan scoots his chair closer to me, whiskey glass in hand. Whiskey is *not* for me; I feel drunk just smelling it on his breath.

"Are you kidding? It's been amazing. I'd say we all got pretty lucky meeting each other!" I say.

"Well, isn't that the truth? I feel pretty damn lucky right about now." He leans in slightly and gives me a smile—one that shows off his dimples. He really is charming, and I'm sure that smile earns him a new girlfriend every week. But he's not the one who put these butterflies in my stomach.

I let out a nervous laugh and offer him a small smile in return. "Yeah, me too. Hanging out with you guys has added so much fun to our trip—honestly. It's amazing we all get along so well."

He takes a sip of his drink and is about to start a conversation with Angus when he turns back to me, as if he wants to say something before he forgets it.

"Hey! If you have a free night this week, I'd love to take you to dinner. I know of a great Italian place."

He doesn't say it quietly, and suddenly we have the attention of everyone at the table, including Jack, who almost looks like he's in pain.

"Ooooh, is someone going on a date?" Callie asks.

"Noooo," I answer quickly with a smile. "Lachlan is just showing off his knowledge of all the hidden gems Paris has to offer. We love Italian food, *right girls?*"

A smile flits across Lachlan's face as he raises a toast to the group. We both know that invitation was intended only for me, for him to take me out on a real date. And because I'm awkward and I don't want to hurt his feelings by turning him down in front of everyone, I figured my best next step was to pretend like I didn't know he was asking me out.

Jack's head is bowed over his lap now, and he's fidgeting with his napkin.

He must be able to feel my gaze on him, because he looks up at me, face serious and eyes intense. He gives me a kind, full smile, but I see something like hurt in his eyes. Or is it annoyance?

I can't tell.

All I know is that I would give anything to know what Jack Thompson is thinking right about now. I find myself wondering that a lot lately.

"Kaia?"

I look up from my book and lock eyes with Jack, and I have to orient myself for a second.

"Jack, hey," I said, closing my book, marking my place with a napkin and taking my feet off of the second chair at my table. "What are you doing here?"

Keeping both hands in his pockets, he gestures an elbow toward the front door of the adorable cafe I've been sitting outside of for the past couple of hours.

"Oh, I uh, had the best croissant of my life here the other day, and I came back for more," he chuckles.

I can't blame him. The croissants here are some of the best I've had so far during my time in Paris.

We both start to speak at the same time, and he laughs, telling me to go ahead.

Through a laugh, I say, "You can join me if you want," and gesture to the seat my feet have just vacated.

Bad idea, Kaia.

"You sure? I don't want to intrude on your reading."

He looks at the book I've just closed on the top of my table, artfully crooked and placed beside my cafe au lait, an Instagram picture waiting to happen.

"No intrusion at all! I was just finishing up," I lie.

Actually, I was in the middle of one of the most action-packed chapters in the whole book so far, but…close enough.

I got out of the Airbnb early this morning to come have a coffee in Montmartre and read for a bit before the day starts, and I've been here by myself for long enough that I'd enjoy the company.

"Great, I'll just…" He pulls the chair out to sit, and we're saved from what was about to be a potentially awkward silence by our server arriving to take Jack's order.

Jack ends up ordering two croissants for good measure before he leans back in the chair. He's been fidgeting with his napkin nonstop since he sat, and I wonder if he feels as awkward as I do. Or maybe he's uncomfortable because I'm being so awkward.

Get it together, Kaia!

"Sorry," he mutters. "I can't help but do this every time there's a napkin in front of me."

I glance at his hands to find him holding an intricate napkin rose… a rose that looks like an exact replica of the one Lachlan gave me the night we all met in the pub.

"It was you," I whisper, quickly realizing I said that out loud and not in my head like I meant to.

"What?" He says it like he has no idea what I'm talking about, but the smile on his lips says differently.

It's a smile that I'll never be able to forget. A smile I shouldn't love as much as I do.

I clear my throat and say, "The, um, napkin rose Lachlan gave me that night we all met…you made it?"

"Oh. yeah, that's right. I almost forgot Lachlan gave you that." He clears his throat with a gruff laugh, but somehow, his words ring false. After a short pause, he adds, "My mom used to make these all the time. Like—all the time. Anytime we went out to dinner as a family, she would ask for extra napkins and make them for my sister and me. Eventually, we learned how to make them as well."

He goes silent, but the air is heavy with something left unsaid.

"She passed three years ago." He looks up at me as the words leave his lips, and I can see the deep pain in his eyes at the memory.

As if my hand has a mind of its own, I reach over and place it over his. His skin is warm, a warmth that radiates up the length of my arm. I glance at his face, registering the undeniable look of shock, I quickly pull my hand back and cross my arms to prevent any further stupidity on my part.

"Jack…I'm so sorry. I'm sure she was an amazing

mom. She had to be to raise you." I point to the rose he just made. "It was really sweet of her to make these for you and your sister."

He looks down at the tangible memory of his mom in his hands, and a contagious smile crosses his face.

"She was." He pauses, then says, "I honestly think you guys would've gotten along really well."

Okay, how do I not overthink that?

I can't keep the blush from creeping up to my cheeks.

"I just know I would've loved her," I say, little more than a whisper. "And thank you for sharing that part of your life with me. I know it's not easy to talk about that stuff."

He looks up from the rose he's holding and hands it to me.

"Hey, I'm sorry…about the other night. I was a bloody jerk, and for no reason. And you…you were caught in the crossfire of Grumpy Jack."

I giggle at the fact that he just referred to himself as Grumpy Jack, and gently take the rose from him. Knowing the history of them makes this one all the more special. And the fact that this one was given to me by Jack? Well, let's just say that makes this rose one of my new prized possessions.

"Grumpy Jack is fully forgiven," I say, and leave it at that, but I *want* to ask him why he was so upset. I want to know if it's because of Lachlan. But I don't ask, because I'm afraid the answer will complicate things.

He smiles and taps on the table like he's contemplating something. Standing up, he puts his arm out, gesturing for me to loop my arm through his. "Let's go for a walk, ya?"

My stomach does that thing it seems to only do when Jack is around. I smile up at him and give him a quick nod since I don't trust my words right now. I throw my book in my purse before standing and threading my arm through his. My whole body responds to the proximity, and I am immediately warm simply by having him next to me.

We make our way through the streets of Montmartre, and I'm taken aback by the architecture, the quaint balconies of wrought iron, and flowers… there are flowers everywhere you look. Walking through this perfect village in the corner of Paris, my arm through Jack's, I feel like I'm dreaming.

Sacré-Cœur peeks out from behind the trees, and memories of me and Jack in the stairwell flood my brain. It takes everything in my power to control my breathing.

"You okay?" Jack must sense my introspection, and I realize I haven't said anything in a while.

I laugh, "Yeah, I—sorry, I was just taking it all in."

"No apologies needed. I get it." He looks around the city street, and we pass by a man on the street playing the saxophone, very well I might add, surrounded by a crowd of adoring fans.

"What's been your favorite part of Paris so far?"

Meeting you.

I keep that one to myself and give him another truth.

"Probably the way it makes me feel. I feel…a renewed sense of excitement for life here. It's getting increasingly difficult to come to terms with the fact that I'll have to leave soon."

A glint of sadness sparks across his face, and it matches the emotion in my chest. We've all become so close during this trip, it doesn't surprise me that he'd be a little sad to see me go. Butterflies whirl in my stomach at the thought.

He stops and turns to face me. He looks serious, more serious than I've seen him since we met.

"Kaia—" he starts, just as a cool drop of rain hits my arm. I turn my palms to the sky and quickly realize that it isn't a drizzle, it's a downpour. I attempt to cover my head with my sweater and let out a sound that's somewhere between a laugh and a yelp.

"Come on!" Jack yells, and grabs onto my hand, pulling me in the direction of a nearby building.

We dodge passersby also running for shelter, among those who came prepared and have already opened their umbrellas.

We find cover under the awning of what looks to be an abandoned shop. The windows are covered with old newspaper, and the signs that used to mark the windows are faded and scraped off.

My once-perfectly curled hair is now a soaked and tangled mess. Thanks to the rain, Jack's hair is stuck to his forehead, but he's still handsome as ever.

Because of course, he looks like that after getting caught in the rain.

"That came out of nowhere," he chuckles, and I realized at that moment he's still holding my hand.

I won't let go if you won't, I think to myself.

Almost as if he can read my mind, he looks down at where our hands are entwined. He gently moves his thumb once over the back of my hand; a simple gesture, loaded with emotions I'm not sure he intends for me to feel. But I do. I can't help it.

"I don't want you to leave," he blurts.

I stare up at him, searching his face for what prompted him to say that. I'm surprised when I don't find a hint of regret for those words that made my heart race.

I stay silent, unsure of what to say. Unsure whether I want him to know exactly how much I don't want to leave either, and how much of that has to do with him.

"Sorry, I, uh…I didn't mean to make it weird," He lets go of my hand.

Paris must have an effect on my bravado because I take it back.

"I'm going to miss you, that's all," he says.

"You are?" I ask, unable to hide the disbelief in my voice.

His expression is equal parts confused and hurt.

"Are you kidding?" He steps closer to me and squeezes my hands. "Kaia, of course, I'm going to miss you."

The rain is increasing in intensity, and my body must just now be registering the drop in temperature because I start to shiver. Jack hesitates before moving his hand up and down along my arms in an attempt to warm them before taking off his jacket and throwing it over my shoulders, which changes this moment from friendly to romantic in two seconds flat.

Our gazes lock and hold, and I want to say something but my teeth start chattering.

He pulls me close, into a hug, rubbing my back to try and warm me up. It's working; I'm much, *much* warmer…but it has nothing to do with him rubbing my back and everything to do with the fact that my face is pressed up against his muscular chest, and he smells heavenly, and being this close to him makes me so happy and nervous that my body doesn't know how to react.

"I'm feeling much warmer," I say as I pull away a little and look back up at him. "Thank you, Jack."

We're so close that his breath warms my skin. I must be dreaming, because the longer our eyes remain locked, the closer he leans in.

I'm *not* dreaming.

He closes the distance between us until his lips hover over mine. If I leaned my body slightly forward, his lips would be on mine. My heart dares me to do it, but my mind deploys some much-needed common sense.

However, I don't pull away. We stay in what feels like a moment suspended in time, rain pouring down around us, and I swear we're the only two people in the world right now.

I like it that way.

I like Jack.

I can't deny that anymore. I don't *want* to deny that anymore. He's magnetic, and I can't pull myself away from him.

Jack moves his hand up to cup my cheek. His touch is so soft, so gentle, so intimate. My skin buzzes with energy, coming alive beneath his touch.

Kiss me. Kiss me.

A car zooms past, spraying rain in our direction and jolting Jack from the trance he seemed to be in. He quickly takes a big step back, running his fingers through his hair.

"I'm so sorry, Kaia…I don't know what I was thinking. That won't happen again."

What if I want it to happen again?

"Jack, it's okay—you didn't do anything wrong." I reach for his hand but he pulls away.

"Lachlan–" he starts, but I cut him off.

"I don't want Lachlan." The words burst out of my mouth like they couldn't bear being unsaid for one more second.

I place my arms around myself and smooth my hands down my arms. "I'm sorry, I didn't mean for that to come out that way. I just…want to make it clear that I'm not interested in Lachlan romantically. I think he's gonna make some girl out there really lucky one day, but I'm just not that girl."

Jack's expression says he's confused, like he didn't think my not being interested in Lachlan was even in the realm of possibility.

"Jack…Lachlan, and I are just friends. That's all we'll ever be…" I let the words trail off, and part of me hopes he can complete my thought so I don't have to say it out loud. Because if I do, it becomes real, and everything changes.

…because I want you.

CHAPTER 13: JACK

Waking up this morning, a realization smacked me right in the face at the same time the sun peeking through the blinds did; the same exciting, and nerve-wracking realization that I had before falling asleep last night: I almost kissed Kaia.

The same Kaia that my best friend is *obviously* pursuing. The girl I've known for less than a month. I got caught up in the moment, and I almost kissed her. I really wanted to kiss her, too. I probably would've gone through with it, had I not been jolted out of whatever state of hypnosis the rain and Kaia's beautiful smile put me under. I blame Paris for being so damn romantic.

I rub my eyes, not wanting to get out of bed yet,

but rolling away from the sun as I try to focus on thoughts about my day ahead, and not on the way my hands felt on Kaia's back, or the way she smelled like brown sugar, or how even soaking wet she was the most beautiful girl I've ever seen. Try and *fail*.

I should've known when I ran into her at the cafe yesterday that I was in trouble. She looked so beautiful, taking up two chairs at the table and focusing on her book. She looked stunning even after running through the torrential downpour. Her copper hair was soaked, and her makeup had run underneath her eyes from the rain, but I was a goner. Undone and utterly at her mercy.

When I noticed she was cold, I didn't even think twice about reaching for her. I acted purely on instinct, like it was a reflex to pull her into my arms. To take away her discomfort. But the proximity and her soft skin under my touch did me in. It's been hard enough to stay away from her in a group, so getting to spend time with her one-on-one felt like a dream come true, as well as a living nightmare, knowing that may have been our only alone time together.

I groan, mentally kicking myself for not kissing her, consequences be damned.

I roll over to check the time right as my phone lights up with a new text message, and a smile spreads across my face when I read the name.

```
Kaia: Hey, it's Kaia! Just wanted
to say thank you again for your
company at the cafe yesterday. We hope
you guys have a blast at the game
today!
```

A very friendly text. Neutral, safe.

So what if I almost kissed her, and then proceeded to give her my phone number? So what if I find myself wanting to talk to her all the time and somehow gravitate toward her in every group setting? We're friends. Friends give each other their phone numbers. I rub a hand over my face and type a quick response, sending it before I have a chance to overthink it.

```
Me: No problem, Kaia! It was fun
hanging for a bit, and I didn't even
have to shower when I got home.
```

I read it fully after sending it, immediately wishing I somehow had a redo, and desperately hoping she knows that's a reference to the rainstorm and not an odd confession of my hygiene routine.

I didn't even have to shower? Who says that?

I groan, my elbow over my eyes to block the sun and my shame from complete lack of game.

Her response interrupts my inner spiral.

Kaia: Haha, me neither! Thank you, monsoon season. I packed shampoo in my purse today, just in case.

I smile, feeling seen and understood. All embarrassment about my former text is *mostly* forgotten as I read her response, the warmth of her charm palpable through the phone.

I'm about to respond again when my door jolts open and Angus comes barreling through, two coffee mugs in hand. I quickly turn my phone screen off and throw my phone on the bed like it's a bomb about to detonate.

Angus stops in front of me, eyes narrowing as he extends one of the mugs in my direction. "Whatcha up to, mate?" He leans over and peeks behind me to where my phone is now laying, screen side down, on the bed.

I take the cup and nod in thanks. "Not much. Just about to get up and get ready for the day." I say nonchalantly.

My phone buzzes, and I immediately wonder if it's Kaia. And by wonder I mean, I really *hope* it's Kaia.

Angus's gaze doesn't leave mine, and his mouth twitches upward in amusement. "You gonna get that, mate? Don't wanna leave her hanging," he says as he turns to walk out of the room.

"*Her* who? It's probably just my dad."

"Mhm, whatever you say, mate!" he yells from the other room.

I roll my eyes and shut my door again, thankful that Angus brought me coffee, though slightly annoyed he thinks he knows everything. But I guess it's only annoying because he's right.

I sit on the edge of the bed and stretch to grab my phone, checking my text messages again.

It is from Kaia. She sent a picture of the napkin rose I gave her yesterday resting in a pot of real roses on the dining table at their Airbnb.

```
Kaia: Knew this vase was missing
something.
```

CHAPTER 14: KAIA

"Right this way, Mademoiselles." An older man in a tux escorts us into a very small elevator inside the most beautiful restaurant I've ever stepped foot in. The scent of sandalwood fills the small space, and I admire the wallpaper intricately designed with nondescript silhouettes.

The girls and I planned to have one *fancy* Michelin Star dinner while we were here, and tonight's the night.

The elevator lurches upward, and we silently share a smile about the fact that we're all shoved in this tiny elevator, dressed to the nines, about to have the most expensive meal of our lives.

The elevator stops shortly after, and the server

escorts us to a perfectly set table. Immediately, I realize I don't know what utensil to use when or for what portion of the meal. We sit down and giggle at each other.

I can't believe we're here.

We order our drinks, and they're brought to our table along with some complimentary, and very, very fancy, appetizers. I had no idea what we ate, but I can tell you that whatever it was, it was delicious.

My phone buzzes in my purse, and I pull it out quickly to read the notification: a new text message from Jack.

My stomach jumps in the best way, and a slow grin spreads across my face.

`Jack: Hope you guys have a wonderful fancy-schmancy dinner,` the text reads.

I respond quickly and put my phone away before I get interrogated about why I'm smiling so much.

`Me: Thank you! Currently eating bread that probably costs more than my car.`

I lift my head to find all three of the girls already staring at me…with knowing smiles on their faces.

"What?" I say, feigning ignorance.

"Um, don't play dumb, Kai! We all see that bright smile on your face," Callie says.

"Could this possibly have anything to do with a golden-haired Aussie whose name rhymes with *crack*?" Adelina asks, taking another bite of her piece of the table bread, eyes locked on mine.

"Whoever could you be referring to?" I joke. "Look, Jack and I have been texting a little bit, but it's just friendly. No big deal."

"Well, that smile on your face was *not* no big deal, but whatever you say," Havannah chimes in with a smile.

I quickly change the subject, asking what everyone's going to order because I have no idea. The girls reluctantly indulge me, and we all chat about our order options and collectively decide what we're getting so we can try a little bit of everything.

We chat to ourselves, taking sips of our overpriced —but very delicious—drinks and pretending we come here every weekend. A pianist plays beautiful classical music in the middle of the dining room. I'm admiring his talent when a slight mechanical sound interrupts.

Adelina gasps, and I turn to see her pointing at the

ceiling. Following her gaze, I look up to find the literal ceiling opening to the dreamy and perfectly blue Parisian sky above us. Birds are flying by the passing clouds while we're eating dinner. *What is life right now?*

On instinct, I take my phone out, snap a picture, and send a quick text to Jack.

Me: The ceiling of the restaurant just opened up to an insane view of the sky, in case you were wondering how much cooler my night is compared to yours.

I follow it up with a smiley face with a tongue sticking out.

Jack: The ceiling…what? You're joking.

Me: Dead serious.

Jack: Well, not to one-up your fancy pants dinner but…I did have grilled cheese for dinner tonight.

Me: GRILLED CHEESE? Well, that's all that needs to be said. There's nothing better than grilled cheese.

Jack: That's what I'm saying. To cure your FOMO, I owe you a homemade Jack's specialty: grilled cheese and

cheesy tomato soup. Next time you're
craving one, I got you, mate.

Me: You're the best, you know that?

I type and send that last message before I could
talk myself out of it. I probably shouldn't have said it,
but…well, I meant it, and I wanted to say it. This trip
is all about having fun, so I'm trying to lean into that
a little more, and a little flirting never hurt anyone.

The realization of my feelings for Jack rises to the
surface at that thought. I know darn well that how I
feel about him goes further than a little flirting, but
I'm not ready to admit that. Not yet. Maybe not ever.
So, for now, harmless flirting it is.

The bubble that indicates someone is typing pops
up in our chat, but it quickly goes away, and I start to
worry that maybe I shouldn't have said that.

Then, a message comes through from Jack.

Jack: You know, I was just thinking
the same thing about you.

I can't help the grin that's plastered on my face,
and decide I should probably put my phone away for
a bit and focus on dinner.

We enjoy the rest of our dinner, taking bites and
passing our plates around like it's Thanksgiving and

not a fancy dinner in Paris. I ended up getting the pork chop, and it was delicious, but nothing compared to the fettuccine alfredo that Callie ordered. We all kept coming back to her plate, so much so that she had to defend her meal with her fork all night.

The server comes over with our checks after our plates have been cleared, and my stomach does a tiny somersault at the total price. Before I freak out about how financially impractical this meal was, I remember that I saved some money specifically for this, and it calms my nerves a bit.

We pay for our meals before following another server back to the elevator. When we reach the street again, we wind up asking one of the valet attendants if they'd take a picture of us. He was more than happy to, and even happier to jump in a selfie with us.

"So, what's next? The night is young!" Havannah says and does a quick twirl with her arms spread wide.

Yeah, we've had a little bit of champagne.

I take approximately two seconds to consider before I say, "Let's go get tattoos!"

We all look at each other in silent excitement.

"I'm calling the Uber now. Where are we headed?" Callie says with a smile.

Before the Uber arrives, I call ahead to make sure they take walk-ins. They said they had a couple of chairs open and that we could stop by any time, so I have the Uber drop us off there.

We walk in, and I'm buzzing with excitement and a little bit of nervousness.

"*Bonjour!*" A tattooed woman greets us at the front and asks what we'd like to get tattooed. On the way over, Callie drew a quick design on an old receipt she had in her purse. A simple *c'est la vie* in a pretty font.

"*Très mignon,*" the woman says with a smile. She introduces herself as Céline, the shop owner. She waves us back to one of the tattoo chairs. We vote for Adelina to go first because she has zero nerves. The rest of us need a couple of minutes to gather our courage.

While Céline sets up, I pull out my phone to take a picture. Adelina closes her eyes and puts a cheesy grin on her face, posing perfectly. I snap a quick picture of her and a couple of the tattoo parlor aesthetics.

"That's a winner," I tell her with a giggle.

Before putting my phone away, I go to my

messages and send a quick text to Jack, a picture of the wall of the tattoo parlor. It's covered, floor to ceiling, with pictures of past tattoos they've done.

Jack: YOU'RE GETTING A TATTOO? Kaia Griffen, now I really am jealous of the night you're having.

He adds, My name is spelled J-A-C-K, in case you need that for your tattoo.

I throw my head back in laughter, and Callie shoots me a questioning glance. I flash her my phone screen, letting her read the text, and she gives me a sly smile back, her eyebrows raising.

I roll my eyes with a grin and return my attention to my phone.

Me: Oh, phew. Thanks for the clarification, I had been spelling it wrong this whole time.

He responds with a smiley face, followed by, Whatcha getting?

Me: No spoilers. You'll have to wait to find out!

Jack: Deal. I can't wait to see it, Kaia girl.

I stare at the screen, blinking rapidly, unsure that I read that correctly. *Kaia girl.* A nickname.

A nickname that shouldn't feel so intimate, but coming from Jack, it's the most intimate, and I don't know why. He only called me Kaia girl.

It's because you're crazy about him, my heart wills me to admit.

I type, Ok, be honest. Would Vin Diesel's face as a tattoo look better on my back or my calf?

Jack immediately responds.

Jack: HAHAHAHA. You got actual tears out of me with that one. Followed by, Calf. Definitely calf.

Me: That's what I was thinking. Also, which one of these is not like the other?

I attach a selfie of me in front of the wall of tattoo art and accompanying decor, trying to fully capture the juxtaposition of me in a frilly pink dress in the middle of a badass tattoo parlor, complete with a cheesy smile and a thumbs-up. The drinks from dinner make me bold enough to cross the threshold from texts to sharing a picture.

He doesn't respond right away, and I start to get nervous that maybe I shouldn't have sent it. I tap my foot nervously and try to focus on what's going on around me and not my phone. After what feels like hours, but was probably only thirty seconds in reality, my phone buzzes.

Jack: You're beautiful.

I blink a few times, making sure I read that correctly, my heart swelling, a blush creeping higher in my cheeks with every reread syllable.

And you look right at home in that tattoo shop, he adds.

I hear the tattoo gun stop and look up to see Céline wiping the extra ink from Adelina's arm to reveal her tattoo. It's perfect. Dainty and beautiful, exactly like we'd envisioned it.

"Who's up next?" Céline asks in a thick French accent.

"I can go," I say, deciding I should before I lose my nerve. I have several tattoos already, but I always get nervous whenever I get a new one.

Céline pats the chair, inviting me to sit. I roll up my sleeve to reveal my forearm and point to where I've decided to place the tattoo.

"*Es-tu prêt?*" she asks, and I find myself admiring the French language as I do almost every time I hear someone speak it. And thanks to my minimal French language learning on Duolingo, I gather that she's asking me if I'm ready.

"*Oui*!" I say with a smile.

CHAPTER 15: KAIA

According to him, Lachlan's birthday is always an *extra* special occasion. He likens the importance of his celebration right up there with a movie premiere or an awards ceremony. His love of partying is nothing new, but a birthday party in Lachlan's honor is icing on the cake—pun intended. Apparently, for his birthday extravaganza last year, he rented out an entire bowling alley for him, Angus, and Jack. Guess how many games they played? One. Angus and Jack said they spent the rest of the evening eating bowling alley pizza and wrangling Lachlan off of the lanes so they wouldn't get kicked out.

We have the honor of being invited to the festivities this year. The party is being held in a speakeasy, which honestly sounds like so much fun, and we were instructed to wear our *fanciest pants,* per the invite from Lachlan. Tell me that's not the most ambiguous dress code of all time.

And because that was the only instruction for dress code, I'm now panic-changing my outfit every five minutes because I can't decide what's too fancy, or what isn't fancy enough. Ahead of time, I laid out three outfit options to choose from. The first is a long-sleeved, army-green, velvet mini dress. It's cute, but I have a feeling my inherently sweaty underarms might pay the price as the night went on. The second option, a black, sequined jumpsuit, is also cute but still didn't have me feeling quite right. It took "fanciest pants" a little too literally.

This brings me to the third option, the one I'm currently modeling in front of the only floor-length mirror in the Airbnb. It's a rainbow, sequined mini dress paired with my favorite white combat boots, making it the perfect glam with a side of grunge. It also has short sleeves to show off my new tattoo. I look like a rainbow disco ball, and I couldn't be happier about it.

I smooth down a few stray hairs as I pull my hair into my signature slicked-back bun, and put in a pair of dainty gold hoop earrings, finally surrendering the mirror to Lina so she can put the finishing touches on her outfit.

I pace around the living room, my stomach doing backflips as I think about the implications of tonight.

I'm going to see Jack.

After getting caught in the rain with him and our *almost* kiss, not to mention the flirty texts we've been exchanging, I'm anxious about being in the same space as him again. I have so much fun with him, and texting him feels like texting someone I've known for years.

And I guess maybe that's the problem, and why I'm so nervous to be around him tonight. I have a lot on my plate right now, and this trip will inevitably come to an end soon, and I'll return home and hopefully find a job. A foreign romance is the last thing I need. And it's easier to remember that when I'm not in the same room as Jack.

Because when I *am* in the same room as Jack, I can't help but gravitate toward him, like we're connected by some invisible string. So, I give myself the pep talk now and build up my resolve while I don't have to look at his devastatingly handsome face…or his sweet smile…or the dimple that appears when he's laughing at something he thinks is really funny.

Okay, I'm not doing such a great job.

I sigh and take one last look in the mirror.

Tonight is gonna be fun, I think to myself. Strictly platonic, no flirting with Jack, fun.

Callie, Havannah, Adelina, and I are having a dance party in the Uber on the way to the party. The driver made the mistake of letting us connect our playlist, so we've been having the time of our lives with Shania Twain, Lady Gaga, old-school Hilary Duff, and Rihanna playing loudly through the speakers.

"Put on some Mike Posner!" Havannah yells excitedly.

"*Mike Posner!*" we all shout in unison.

Our obsession runs deep.

A few years ago, we all went to a dive bar for a

karaoke night. We were a couple drinks in, watching session after session of terrible but entertaining karaoke when the streak was broken by this guy with an *incredible* voice.

He sang Donna Summer's "Last Dance" and absolutely killed it. The whole bar erupted in cheers when he was done, and we all chanted "Encore!" over and over until he sang another song.

As he was singing his second song, Havannah leaned over and shouted over the music, "He's so good! And he kinda looks like Mike Posner, right?"

We all laughed, and I leaned in to get a better look. I blinked a few times as clarity hit me. He looked like Mike Posner because he *was* Mike Posner.

What started as a random girls' night out turned into the night that we had a margarita with Mike Posner and talked about global warming. It remains one of our favorite memories to date.

Though, memories of that night are suddenly overshadowed by the thought of Jack. His hands lingering in mine after we got caught in the rain, electricity pulsing between us. My hands immediately start sweating, and my mouth goes dry.

"Kaia, are you okay? You look spooked,"

Havannah says, concerned.

"I'm okay. I guess I'm just nervous about seeing Jack," I answer honestly.

"When are you guys going to finally admit that you're crazy about each other, ride off into the sunset, and live happily ever after?" she asks as if that is the most obvious plan.

"One, um, never. And two, *happily ever after* doesn't exist," I say, realizing how pessimistic I sound.

"Yeah, yeah, practicality is king, ten-year plan, blah, blah. I get it. Sometimes plans change. Often for the better. Let go tonight, Kai, and have fun with no pressure. You deserve it," she says encouragingly.

The Uber drops us off in front of the speakeasy, and it's almost as if I have to instruct my feet to start moving toward the front door.

Everything's okay, I remind myself. I can say hi to Jack in passing and mind my own business the rest of the night. Easy, peasy, lemon squeezy.

Who am I kidding? This is hard, hard, lemon freaking hard.

When we walk inside, we are immediately greeted by a man dressed as a hotel bellhop.

"Checking in?" he asks in perfect English.

"We are," Callie giggles.

"Do you have a reservation?" He consults the large log book on the desk in front of him.

"We do. It's under 'Lach-ness,'" Lina says, giving the password that was printed on the invitation.

"Of course, madams, right this way."

He ushers us through what looks like a wardrobe. Once inside, he pushes against the back wall and it opens up into a hallway, lit only by candle sconces hanging on the wall.

"Have a wonderful evening, ladies," he says and shuts the door behind him, leaving us alone in this mysterious corridor.

After a few seconds of walking in almost-complete darkness—which makes me only slightly anxious that we were suddenly thrust into a horror film—the speakeasy came into view and…*wow*.

I'm immediately blown away by the beauty of this place.

"Woah, where are we?" Callie says, as mesmerized as I am.

The room isn't very large—it's exactly the right size for an intimate gathering, without feeling like you're suffocating. The walls are covered with what looks like old newspapers and the ceilings are painted a beautiful navy blue, adorned with stars of various sizes painted in white. It's lit only by the flickering flames of candles and ornate hanging light fixtures shaped like stars.

"I feel like I just stepped into a book," I whisper in awe. "This place is beautiful!"

An arm comes around my shoulders, and I turn to see the birthday boy.

"Aww, you guys came!"

*And, w*hoa. I smell whiskey, tequila, and maybe a hint of Fireball. I might get drunk simply from being in his proximity.

"Of course, Lach! We wouldn't miss *this*," Adelina says enthusiastically, gesturing to the room at large. "Happy birthday!"

Lachlan goes in for a full hug, which is definitely doubling as a way to hold himself upright.

"You doing okay?" I pull back and look at him, giving him a knowing smile.

"Oh ya, mate! I'm doing fantastic—it's my birthday, didn't you hear?" He throws both of his arms out with a huge grin, a gesture that must've thrown him off balance because he stumbles as if he might fall at any second.

All four of us girls crowd around him in case we have to catch him if he goes down.

"Coming through," Angus says, slinging Lachlan's arm over his shoulder to steady him. "I got him!"

He must have started drinking way before we got here. Don't get me wrong, Lachlan is always a party, but even that night in the pub I didn't see him this wobbly, and the evening has barely begun.

"Ah, my best mate," he says dreamily to Angus. "What would I do without you?"

"In this present moment, you'd fall on your bum and embarrass yourself on your birthday. Can't have that now can we?" Angus laughs.

Something in the air changes as Jack walks over, his simple, "Hey," sending chills up my arms.

He has on a well-cut suit, and I'm confident I've never seen a more attractive human in my life. The white shirt under his jacket is unbuttoned a bit, and another of his tattoos peeks through. It looks like it may be a ship sitting atop rough waves, right over his heart, and I immediately want to know the story behind it.

His sandy hair is beautifully disheveled, and his

cheeks have that quintessential blush to them like he's been out in the sun. The same thing I noticed the very first night I saw him.

"Shall we?" He gestures toward the bar.

I'll admit it, this night is going *much* better than I anticipated. Everyone is getting along, Lachlan is behaving himself—despite being hammered the second we walked in—and Jack and I have had minimal face-to-face contact. The girls and I are discussing which cafe we want to have breakfast at in the morning while sipping our French 75s.

I glance up from my phone and the Yelp list of best brunches in Paris I was skimming, to find a very wobbly Lachlan climbing on top of the big, rectangular table in the middle of the room. Jack and Angus, smiling and shaking their heads, walk over and put their arms out, as if to catch him when he inevitably goes tumbling off the table. Lachlan taps a metal fork against his beer bottle to get the attention of everyone at the party, and the volume of the techno music playing in the background is lowered.

I look around, searching for a DJ, but there's no

one to see. A nice touch to the speakeasy ambiance, I'll admit.

"Thank you all for coming to celebrate me, and I'm really happy you all love me because I'm so great," Lachlan says with a cheeky smile and a wink. At least, that's what I think he said. He's slurring his words, and his accent is so thick right now that it's hard to tell.

"I especially want to thank my gal, Kaia, for being such a great friend. Great, great friend. Just a jolly old *friend*," he says.

Well, that's a little bit odd. I wasn't expecting him to say that.

A mix of emotions swirls in my chest: gratitude for the shout-out, embarrassment at being put on the spot, but mostly confusion because he's talking about me and not his two best friends who he's known for years. I tilt my head and shoot him a questioning but amused look. The girls are watching me, giggling behind their hands and thoroughly entertained.

"Funny story friends," He clinks his glass unnecessarily again. "I'm pretty sure I'm in love with her."

The room goes silent. Smiles turn to slack-jawed

shock and my face flushes.

"That woman right over there. She's the greatest woman I've ever met, but she doesn't love me. She doesn't love me," he slurs. "She's *actually* keen on my best friend." He looks down from the table toward Angus.

"Not you." He turns abruptly toward Jack, almost falling off the table. "There he is! That's right—Kaia's keeping her heart for my boy Jack-Jack. She's never told me, but I can tell by the way she looks at him. She's looking at him while I'm looking at her." He accentuates this by pointing from Jack to me, sloshing his beer in the process.

"I see it every time we're all together. Can't say that I blame her. It'd probably be cute if I wasn't mad about her myself but hey…what can you do, you know?"

I'm frozen. Shocked. Sure that I'm dreaming. I must be. There's no way Lachlan is airing this all out in front of a room full of people.

Except my ears won't stop ringing, and my heart pounds dangerously fast in my chest. This is real life. The room is silent, except for the faint sound of the music, and I can feel eyes on me. I don't look to make sure, but I'm confident Jack is staring right at me.

What the actual hell, Lachlan? I think to myself.

This drunk idiot thinks he's *in love* with me? I don't think Lachlan would know love if it slapped him across his perfectly-tanned face, which is exactly what I feel like doing right this second.

Who does he think he is, putting me—and Jack, *his best friend*—on blast like that? I'm mortified and angry, and I can't sit here any longer.

Angus and Jack quickly jump up to pull Lachlan off the table and take him to the restroom. As soon as they are out of sight, I stand and grab my purse, wishing I could teleport my way out of here before I stop and chug the rest of my drink.

Only then do I march toward the exit, and I don't even have to check—I know the girls are right behind me.

CHAPTER 16: JACK

Lachlan throws his arm around my shoulder and pulls me close.

"It's love," he slurs. "Kaia is love you."

That was almost a sentence. On his breath is the heavy scent of every alcoholic beverage he's had tonight.

Ignoring his ramblings, and trying not to be mad at him for embarrassing Kaia, I readjust him under my shoulder.

"All right. Let's get ya home, huh?"

"What? The party just started!" He tries to wiggle out of mine and Angus's grips to make his way back into the party, which was over the second the girls left. Everyone else awkwardly and silently followed their lead.

"It's just us, mate."

He must think he's moving much faster than he is, because he barely makes it one step away from us before we're back under his arms, hoisting him up to keep him from planting face-first on the floor.

"Fine, to the after-party!" he shouts, and I roll my eyes, knowing the after-party will be Lachlan passed out on his bed.

Angus and I haul him out of the speakeasy after handing the man in the bellhop uniform the black card from Lachlan's wallet. I try not to look at the total for the reservation as we help Lachlan sign the receipt. His app has been successful, but sometimes I think Lachlan is a little *too* adventurous with his spending.

While we wait for our Uber, my brain won't stop replaying the entire scene of Lachlan's little public speech fiasco in my head.

"*Love*" he had said. That's mad. Kaia and I have only known each other for a few weeks.

But the look on her face, when Lachlan dropped that bomb on the whole party, hinted that there might be some truth to it. The look on her face didn't say,

"Lachlan, that's ridiculous." It said, *"Lachlan, why the hell would you say that out loud?"*

I don't have long to meditate over what to think as our ride pulls up to Lachlan's apartment, a cream-colored Parisian dream.

This is what I mean about adventurous spending, but QuestFriends Guild, his company, is picking up the tab so here we are. I throw Lachlan on the couch a little more roughly than I intended to. Though I do want to punch him for embarrassing Kaia, I also want to ask him a million clarifying questions to find out how he knows she loves me and what I should do about it. Instead, I bring him a bottle of water and a bin should he need to release the alcohol from his system before morning.

I can't say that I'm surprised by how tonight ended. Lachlan's birthday parties are almost sure to end in chaos, and Angus and I are always here to pick up the pieces. I'm sure he'll feel like crap in the morning, both because of his raging hangover and for how he called out Kaia. Lachlan is a lot of things, but he's no bully. Tonight was all alcohol talking, not that it excuses his behavior.

I tell Angus I'm gonna head to sleep, and he

refrains from mentioning anything about Kaia—probably understanding that I'm very much still processing. After closing myself in Lachlan's guest room and changing into more comfortable clothes, all I can do is sit on the bed, my hands folded and leg bouncing up and down, as I replay Lachlan's words over and over again. Not every word, only the important ones. The ones that declared Kaia's in love with me.

What do I do with that?

Those words weigh heavily on my mind, while also being equally light and distant. I'm honestly spiraling. Is it true? Or was Lachlan just being…Lachlan? Her reaction pointed to the former, but I don't want to assume.

And…do I want it to be true?

The image of her, cheeky smile and thumbs up in a beautiful pink dress, standing in the middle of a tattoo shop, floats into my head. God, she's beautiful. And I couldn't help telling her then.

I think back to the rain storm, both of us soaked to the bone and not an inch of space between us.

I should've kissed her then.

She *wanted* me to kiss her then.

I shake my head, reality settling in. There is undeniably something between us.

Kaia Griffen is *the* girl. The one who, now that I know her, I'm ruined for anyone else. There wouldn't even be room for anyone else with the amount of space she occupies in my mind.

I hear movement by the bedroom door and turn to see Angus standing there, not realizing how much he'd startled me.

"Sorry, mate. The door was open—was gonna see if you wanted a pint."

He holds out a frosted glass already filled with an amber ale.

"Oh, I'm alright. Thanks, mate," I say in response.

Angus takes a sip for himself.

"So, what are you gonna do about it?" Angus asks.

"About…not wanting a pint?"

With that quintessential Angus grin, he says, "No, you daft man. Your feelings for Kaia. I see the way you look at her. We all do. Now, what are you gonna do about it, mate?"

CHAPTER 17: KAIA

The girls indulged me in a wonderful gelato treat to take my mind off Lachlan's public confessional. I got the mint chocolate chip with an extra scoop because if ever there was a double scoop night, it was tonight.

To further distract my mind, Callie led us to the Eiffel Tower, which we had yet to see at night. The lights twinkled beautifully, reflecting in my sequined dress. We sat in a comfortable silence, finishing off our gelato, and enjoying the magic of Paris at night. We didn't talk about what happened because I was still processing. We simply enjoyed the rest of our night, and I couldn't be more thankful for these friends I get to do life with.

After getting back to our Airbnb, I change into comfy clothes, completely wrap myself in a blanket, and plop myself right in bed to watch *New Girl*—my comfort show of choice. In the middle of Nick telling Jess to get her own French toast sticks, I hear a knock at the door of our place. I check the time on my phone—half past eleven.

It's pretty late for visitors, I think.

My bedroom door creaks open, and Adelina peaks her head in with a weary look on her face.

"It's for you…it's Jack," she says.

The panic must've been evident on my face because she walked over and sat on the edge of my bed.

"Take a deep breath. It's okay. I can tell him to leave."

I take a big breath in, get out of bed, and compose myself. "No, it's okay. I can do this."

I look down at my oversized tee shirt, shorts, and fuzzy heart socks I'm wearing halfway up my shins. I throw a questioning look at Lina.

"He's not here to see your outfit, Kaia. He's here to see you. We're here if you need us. I'll send him in."

I held my breath while waiting for him. It was only about thirty seconds before Jack strolls into my room, but it feels like an eternity. I exhale as he steps in and closes the door behind him, looking down at the ground the entire time.

I initially want to step closer to him, but his body language has me retreating until the back of my knees hit the bed.

"Jack, look I—" I start to say, but he jumps in with, "Is it true?"

He looks up at me, the exhaustion is plain on his face. He looks sad, too—but I'm not sure if it's for me or him. His hair is disheveled, one side of his shirt is untucked, and he looks like he's been through hell and back tonight. My guess is he and Angus picked up the pieces from atomic-bomb Lachlan tonight, so I guess he sort of *has* been through hell and back.

He's probably also upset because this little confession has ruined his ability to be my friend. *Perfect.* I'm the crappy friend who couldn't even keep herself from falling in love with him, and now it's all ruined because of my stupid feelings.

I'm being dramatic, but I think I've earned it.

"We don't have to talk about it. It was nothing.

Can we please pretend it never happened?" I say.

Jack locks eyes with me and holds my stare for eternity. He's never looked at me this way before—like he knows the truth and is pleading with me to say aloud all of the things I'm afraid to.

He takes a step closer, never once dropping his gaze from mine.

"No, Kaia. I can't do that."

Another step closer.

"Is it true?" he asks again.

"Why does it matter?" I say, not realizing I've started crying until hot tears stream down my face.

I'm terrified that I'm about to lose him. The fact that I'm absolutely falling for this man undoubtedly ruins our ability to be friends, and I'd rather be secretly in love with him and pretend I'm not than live my life without him in it. If I need to deny my true feelings to keep him in my life, I can do that. I can make it work.

Jack steps even closer until we're practically chest-to-chest. He lifts a hand to my cheek and sweeps away a tear.

Mark that moment as reason number 934,631 why I'm crazy about this man.

He leans closer, and I have to angle my head to look at him. I anticipate a consoling hug from him, but instead, his hands cup the sides of my face. Before I have time to register what the heck is happening, his lips hover over mine.

"It matters because if it's true, I'm going to kiss you like I've wanted to since the moment I saw you for the first time in that pub," he whispers and I feel the warmth of his breath on my skin as he says it.

He kisses my left cheek, and my knees weaken.

His right hand slides around my lower back, pulling me closer and keeping me steady, while his left thumb slides back and forth across my jaw.

"It matters because I think about you *every single day*."

He kisses my right cheek, and I'm breathing so hard my chest is touching his with every inhale.

"It matters because you *consume* my thoughts."

He's so close now that his lips brush mine as he talks. My body doesn't know how to respond. Every point of contact I have with him is electrified. I never want to not be touching him.

"It matters because I'm pretty sure I'm in love with you, Kaia."

I'm stunned, shocked, and convinced that this can't be happening. I've died and gone to heaven. I'm sure Chris Hemsworth is about to walk in, hand me my favorite coffee, and ask if I want to watch reruns of Gilmore Girls.

Jack must register my shock from the look on my face because he pulls back enough to look me directly in the eye and adds, "I mean it. I love you."

"You love me?" I ask in disbelief.

"I love you." He laughs gruffly as he says it. "I'm full-blown, Tom Cruise jumping up and down on a couch in love with you. President of the Kaia fan club. I'm crazy about you."

We've somehow moved, and my back is pressed against the closet door. I can't look away, afraid to break eye contact with him. He puts his hands on either side of my head, eyes scanning my face. His smile has a hint of mischief in it, and I so badly want to know what he's thinking right this second. But I also don't. This man scrambles my brain in the best way possible.

I look up at him, trying to control my breathing. The blend of his cologne envelopes me, making it even harder for me to concentrate.

"Jack, I love you, too," I say, voice barely above a whisper.

The next thing I know, his mouth is on mine in a devastatingly tender but urgent kiss. It feels like coming home. It feels like exactly the feeling I've been chasing since I got here—joy, excitement, exhilaration, every good thing to ever exist, wrapped up in one kiss.

Jack pulls away slightly and I immediately miss his warmth.

No, no, no, come back!

I grip his shirt with both of my hands and pull him closer to me.

"Do you know how long I've wanted to kiss you?" Jack asks and chuckles against my lips.

I smile against his kiss and answer with the truth. "I think I have an idea."

He pulls away and swipes his thumb across my bottom lip.

"You're a dream. I've been pretending like I haven't wanted to kiss you since the moment I met you." He leans in, hovers over my mouth for a second, and kisses me again. "I'm done pretending."

"Good, me too," I say with a smile.

He sighs, and while I hear the contentment in that breath, there's something underneath it as well.

"Listen, I don't want to lose this moment we're in, but I've got something I need to talk to you about," he adds.

I quickly pull back so I can look at him. His face is serious but relaxed, and he's started rubbing his hands up and down my arms in an attempt to squelch the anxiety I'm sure is written all over my face.

"I don't mean to make it a big dramatic moment—it's really not a big deal."

Somehow, his words aren't providing me any comfort. In fact, I'm getting more nervous. "What is it?" I ask, hesitant to know, desperate to stay in the love-sick bubble we've found ourselves in.

He rubs the back of his neck with one hand, the other holding mine. "I have to go home sooner than I thought. Back to Australia."

He pauses to make room for my response, but nothing comes out. I don't know what to say, and what I want to do is rewind time before I knew he had to leave me and go back to kissing him. To stay that way for...I don't know. Forever sounds like a long enough time, I'd say.

Looking down at our hands entwined, he sweeps his thumb across the back of mine—a comforting gesture as he drops a bomb that leaves me devastated.

"I leave in three days."

CHAPTER 18: KAIA

It's been about thirty-six hours since Jack told me he's leaving, not that I'm counting or anything. I'm totally chill. I'm the most chill ever.

It helps that we've spent almost every second together since then. We've been alternating between staying at my Airbnb and Lachlan's place, but he sleeps on the floor because he's so sweet and doesn't want to rush anything or make me uncomfortable.

He keeps saying, "I just want to be near you all the time," and it's devastatingly sweet.

I told him that he didn't have to sleep on the floor, but he insists, so I don't argue.

My phone vibrates with a text from him, pulling me from my daydream.

Hi, pretty girl. Meet you downstairs whenever you're ready. No rush though.

He's meeting me here so we can walk to a cute cafe a couple of blocks from my place. I think that's one of the many things I love about Paris. There are so many cafes, restaurants, and shops within walking distance. And they're all the most charming, adorable places.

I know he said not to rush, but I can't not rush because I'm so excited to see him. I grab my purse, lock up, and practically run down the stairs.

Until I lose my footing on one of the steps and almost fall down the remaining stairs, which slows me down.

The door opens much quicker than I expected, and I fly into Jack's arms.

"Woah, there!" he laughs. "Hi to you, too."

He's still holding me as he smiles and leans down to kiss me.

I don't know how much time has passed because I seem to black out every time Jack kisses me, but eventually, he pulls back and rubs his thumb across my cheek. "You okay?"

"Who, me?" I ask. "I've literally never been better.

Why do you ask?" I say with a laugh and open my eyes to look at him.

He chuckles and makes sure I'm steady on my feet before we head to the coffee shop.

When we arrive and walk inside, the interior is as adorable and charming as the outside. Dark floral wallpaper lines the walls, and vintage, ornate chandeliers hang in every corner. Faint classical music plays over the speakers. This morning's coffee date is already everything I hoped it would be, and it's helping me forget how sad I am that Jack is leaving soon.

Once we order and find a small table in the corner, he reaches across the table to grab my hands and he gives them a small squeeze.

"I love you," he says. I'll never get tired of hearing that.

"I love you, too." I'll never get tired of saying it either.

We sit there, making googly eyes across the table, playing thumb wars in between holding hands, and I'm sure everyone in this cafe is sick of us already. I'm not, though. I'll never get over being loved by Jack Thompson.

Jack gets up to grab our coffees when they call our order number, comes back with my latte, and sets it in front of me. The latte art on top is stunning—a mini Eiffel Tower.

I take out my phone to snap a quick picture and look up to see Jack smiling at me.

"What?" I ask, blushing.

"Just looking at ya," he says.

"Like what you see?" I joke.

His expression turns serious. "I love what I see."

I know he means it, too, and the way that makes me feel is terrifying given the fact that he'll be in another country in two days. A country far, far away from me. Panic rises in my chest, and I quickly take a sip of my latte, trying to shove the feeling down.

"So, what are you and the guys gonna do today?" I ask. Jack, Lachlan, and Angus are having a guy's day before Jack leaves, and knowing this bunch, they're probably doing something crazy.

"I think we're going skydiving."

Of course they are.

"What?" I say, practically spitting my coffee out at him. I make an apologetic face and wipe my mouth with a napkin.

He laughs. "You mean, jumping out of a plane doesn't sound like your idea of fun, my love?"

He has to stop calling me that or I'm never going to let him leave. We'll have to stay here forever, whether he likes it or not.

"No. No, it does not," I say. "But I hope you guys have the best time…and be careful."

He lifts my hand to his mouth and kisses it. "We'll be careful, I promise." Then he asks, "Got any fun plans today while I'm gone?"

"Actually, yeah! I'm on the hunt for some bookstores, and then the girls and I are gonna have dinner tonight."

"Oooh, a day in Parisian bookstores—that sounds like your heaven," he says, smiling and tracing gentle circles on the back of my hand.

"I know. It really is," I agree vehemently.

He chuckles and takes a sip of his coffee.

"I'm gonna miss you today, Kaia girl," he says quietly.

I look up to meet his eyes. "I'm going to miss you, Jack." On the surface, we're talking about today, but I know deep down we both mean when he leaves for Australia. Once again, panic threatens to break free, and I do everything I can to pretend it's not there.

"I feel like I haven't gone more than a couple of hours without kissing you since that first time. What in the world am I going to do for a whole day?" He gives me sad, puppy dog eyes, and I can tell he's trying not to laugh. That lightens my mood a bit.

"Hmm, that does sound like a problem," I say, putting on my best overly-dramatic thinking face. "I guess…you'll just have to make up for it right now."

His face instantly morphs into a grin. Gosh, his smile is something else. It's slightly crooked, and he has the teeniest gap in his front teeth. I'm not being dramatic when I say he's the most handsome man I've ever seen in my life. Sorry, Ryan Reynolds.

"You know what, that's a wonderful idea." He leans over and grabs the leg of my chair. Before I realize what's happening, he quickly scoots me over until I'm right in front of him, my knees nestled between his legs.

"Jack, we're in public." I blush and let out a nervous laugh as he puts his hands on my knees and brings his face to mine. His breath fans across my lips and the heat of his hands on my thighs warms my whole body.

"We're in the city of *love* after all," he says, accentuating the word *love*, "and it's taking everything in me to keep my hands to myself."

Oh yeah, I'm in trouble. Is this cafe on fire, or am I just sweating?

He leans in and whispers in my ear, "Can I kiss you, Kaia girl?" and I'm glad we're in public because it's very much helping—no, *forcing*—us to take things slow.

Enjoy this while it lasts. The words ring in my head, and another wave of panic threatens to overtake me.

"Always," I say, and I mean it. Jack can kiss me anytime, always.

I feel his smile as he leans into me and kisses me slowly. He kisses me in a way that isn't rushed, like he doesn't feel the same time constraint I do given the fact that he leaves soon. He kisses me like we have all the time in the world, but all I can think about is all the time we *don't* have.

He kisses me like he could stay this way forever. And I could, too, but I know we can't.

It has to come to an end eventually, doesn't it? It's too good to be true, right?

CHAPTER 19: JACK

When my dad called me a few days ago and said that my gran had fallen down the stairs in her home and broken a few bones, I didn't hesitate when I told him I'd come home, even though it pained me a bit to cut my trip short. And at that point, my feelings for Kaia were a secret I was trying to pretend didn't exist. Now that I know how she feels, and she knows I feel the same way, leaving is going to be pretty excruciating. But she seems to be handling it well. If she's freaking out at all, she's hiding, because she seems cool, calm, and collected.

It's going to destroy me to say bye to her. When I told her, I almost asked her to come with me, but decided that might be a little too much, too soon for her.

Not for me, though. When it comes to Kaia, I'm all in. She's my Kaia girl, and I'm holding on to her with everything in me.

Family is everything to me, though, and my dad and gran need me right now. My dad insisted that I didn't have to come home, but I told him that I was coming no matter what, and that I'd be there to help him with whatever he needed. He had teared up on the phone at that, and in turn, I teared up as well. Ten minutes later, we're laughing like a couple of idiots at the fact that we're both crying and sniffling into the phone.

When my mom got sick, I sort of shut down. I didn't help as much as I should've. I spent most of the time angry—mostly that I couldn't do anything about it. I couldn't take her sickness away. I couldn't save her. So I got angry, and I shut down. My dad became her full-time caregiver, and I made myself scarce. Seeing her sick hurt too much, and I never wanted to deal with it, so I always filled my calendar with something—work, friends, partying, whatever I could do to avoid being around the house.

And that's why I need to go home. I don't want my

dad to have to do this alone. I want to be there for him, and my gran.

"I'll see you soon, Dad," I told him.

"Thank you, Jacky boy."

I booked my flight home on the morning of Lachlan's birthday party. Which was also the morning before I found out Kaia loves me, otherwise known as one of the best days of my life.

And every second I've spent with her since has also felt like some of the best moments of my life. She's everything. And I know it's just the beginning for us.

I haven't told her this yet, and I'm sort of hoping I've made this clear already, but I don't plan to be away from her for long once I go back to Australia. I've already been planning a trip to America to visit her once she's back from Paris. I just want her to know that I'm so serious about her. About us.

Saying bye to her, and Paris, will be hard. But it's not the end for us. Not even close.

The boys and I have a right ol' guy's day planned today, and for some reason Angus and I let Lachlan pick the activity. We should've known it would be something idiotic or dangerous. Or both.

So, ladies and gents, today we're going skydiving.

The thought of skydiving has never really freaked me out that much. I'm not afraid of heights, but it's also never been on my list of things I would like to do. Not even close.

But Lachlan suggested it, and he's so excited about it, so we figured, what the heck? *C'est la vie, when in Paris*, and any other cliche that's appropriate for this situation.

Before we take off, I pull out my phone to see a text from my girl.

Kaia: Please, please, please be careful today.

You worried about me, love? I say, adding a winky emoji at the end.

She sends back a GIF of Jim from *The Office*, rolling his eyes, and it makes me chuckle.

Kaia: No, it's just…I'll have to eat gelato by myself tomorrow if something happens to you, and eating gelato alone is just not as fun, you know?

Oh, right, right. That makes sense. Well, wouldn't want that now, would we? I respond, adding, I'll be safe, love. I promise.

I put my phone in my pocket and head over to where Lachlan and Angus are signing waivers that state that we—or rather, our family members—can't sue this skydiving company for wrongful death if we die a fiery and tragic death, because we agreed to it.

Once we fill out our paperwork, they hand us these wonderful matching blue jumpers to change into before putting all of our gear on. We look like sticks of Laffy Taffy, and we spend a good ten minutes laughing about it until we're doubled over with tears running from our eyes.

Lachlan steps out of the hangar and does a very exaggerated salute to nothing and no one, saying, "Let's do this, boys!"

He proceeds to skip his way over to the airplane, and I feel like he's way too excited for someone who's about to jump out of a plane, but hey, *c'est la vie*, right?

I follow his lead and skip right on behind him, Angus's laughter fading with the wind as we get closer.

CHAPTER 20: KAIA

I'm on a bit of a high from my day of solo exploring. I mostly explored bookstores, but I popped into a few other shops here and there. I found these adorable friendship necklaces in one of the shops and bought them for all of us girls.

Although, I spent most of my time missing Jack, and it makes me even more nervous about his upcoming departure back to Australia. If I already miss him this much—the ache is a significant weight on my chest—then what the hell am I going to do when he leaves and we're in completely different time zones?

As soon as we parted, he sent me an incredibly sweet text. One that made my chest squeeze—at first in the best way, then because of the mounting anxiety I've been feeling about all of this and how it'll inevitably end.

Jack: Had the best morning with you, beautiful. Counting down the hours until I get to see you again, and if I'm being really honest, I'm haunted by that outfit you wore this morning. In the best way. I can't stop thinking about it. About you.

His texts are like poems, and love songs, written only for me. And that one for sure made me blush.

He added, Hope you have the time of your life whilst Parisian bookstore exploring. Send me pictures. Love you, Kai.

I'm meeting the girls at a pizza shop nearby, and can't wait to tell them about my day, and honestly vent a little about Jack. We all had somewhat of a solo day today. We figured it would be good for the overall trip if we got some time to ourselves and explore something we each individually wanted to see.

My Uber driver drops me off out front of the pizza place and I head inside. The girls beat me there, and there's a seat waiting at their table for me. I see them as soon as I walk in and skip over excitedly. Today was fun, but I missed my girls. They all stand and we do a quick round of hugs before sitting down. Callie slowly slides a glass of champagne in my direction, and I make a big gesture with my hands and silently mouth, "Thank you!"

I'm a sucker for some good ol' dramatics.

The server comes over and takes our order, then we settle in to spill the tea on everyone's day.

Havannah and Callie went to a high tea and climbed the Eiffel Tower.

"I tried meeting up with Jules, but he's been so busy." Callie flashes an expression that's half shy smile, half pout.

Ah, that's right! Her Parisian not-so-boyfriend. They've been texting nonstop, but haven't met up just yet.

Adelina had a picnic at The Luxembourg Gardens, and it sounds like it was a magical day for her as well.

"How was your day, Kai?" Adelina asks, taking a sip of her drink.

"It was good. I explored a few bookstores," I say, rummaging through my bag to pull out the necklaces I bought. "I also got us these!"

I hold up the choker necklace, which has white beads covering the entire string, and a tiny smiley face bead right in the middle.

"Ok, these are so cute," Havannah says as they all grab theirs to put them on.

"I saw these and couldn't leave without them." Famous last words anytime I step into a boutique. Ask anyone that knows me, and they'll confirm.

"You had breakfast with Jacky-boy, right? How'd that go?" Callie asks.

"Oh, yeah! I did," I say, sadness settling in once more, and apparently, it showed all over my face.

"Oh no. What happened?" Callie asks, concerned.

"No, nothing happened. It was a good breakfast. I'm just sad," I say and pause, not really knowing where I'm going with it. I decide I'm just going to be one hundred percent honest about how I feel about everything. I have to.

"I mean, he leaves in two days," I say.

"Yeah, I'm really sorry, Kaia. But thank god for FaceTime, right? You guys will be able to pick right back up where you left off!" Havannah chimes in.

"It's not gonna work," I say before she's even done talking.

They all look at me like they aren't sure they're hearing me correctly.

"What do you mean?" Havannah asks.

"I mean, there's no way it works long-term, right? We live on opposite ends of the world." I say, getting flustered.

"Kaia, that man loves you more than anything. He'd do anything for you. And you love him. I haven't seen you this happy with a man in…I don't know how long." Havannah adds. "Maybe ever."

"Yeah, Kai. You and Jack are the real deal. I can see it. We all can," Callie says.

I look to Adelina, hoping she'll back me up on this. Her responding stare feels like she's looking directly into my soul.

"You're running away," she says, gaze wholly fixed on me.

That one cuts deep. I actually can't believe she said that out loud.

"Running away?" I ask, flinching, sure my shock and hurt flash across my face.

I start talking again before she can respond. "How can you say I'm running away? I'm only pointing out the inevitable conclusion to a pretty reckless situation

I've gotten myself in, and I don't have a damn clue what to do about it."

The words fly from my mouth as if they have a mind of their own. As if they can't possibly stand one more second bottled up inside. "Yes, I love him, okay? I didn't want to. I didn't come to Paris to meet someone, and in fact, I tried to actively avoid it. This thing with Jack turned out to be so much more meaningful to me than I thought was possible. But what does that even matter if we never see each other in person? It's stupid! It doesn't even make any sense. Yeah, we love each other. *So what?* Is that even enough?"

"I think it is," Havannah says, and Callie and Adelina nod in agreement.

I huff a laugh, but it's hurt and humorless.

"You know, I thought you guys were going to have my back on this, I thought you'd—" I start, but Adelina interrupts.

"You thought we'd what, Kaia? Continue to sit back and watch you choose what makes you most comfortable over what actually lights you up inside? You thought we'd just idly stand by while you choose to do what you think other people want you to do or what's practical, even though it slowly sucks the life out of you? Do you know how difficult it is to watch someone you love dearly live their life like that?"

I open my mouth to respond but nothing comes out. I have nothing to say. No rebuttal. I'm speechless. I had no idea she felt this way. How did I miss this?

And where does she get the nerve to say all of this to me right now?

I whip my gaze toward Havannah and Adelina. "Do you both feel this way, too?"

Havannah doesn't wait before nodding. "Yeah, Kai. It's been this way for a while. We've tried to talk to you about it, but you don't listen when it comes to this."

I can't believe what I'm hearing. Callie nods in agreement, and shrugs, because everything that needed to be said already has been.

I scoot my chair out and stand, gathering my things and setting some money on the table to cover my portion of the bill. It's taking everything in me to hold back the tears that are begging to be released.

"Kaia, don't go. Please, just sit, and let's finish talking this out," Havannah says.

No way. I'm done with this conversation for the

night. Maybe the week.

I shake my head. "I'm gonna head home, but I hope you guys have a great rest of your night."

And with that, I take my purse and head out of the restaurant, not entirely sure what direction our Airbnb is. My only thought is to do exactly what Adelina accused me of: run.

I burst out of the restaurant and start walking back to our Airbnb. I planned to stop at some point and call an Uber, but I need the walk to blow off some steam—and I need to cry, too.

The streets are buzzing with people, so I try to conceal it as best I can, but I can't help letting some tears fall.

I'm upset about the fight, but also a little mad at myself because I feel like I could've handled that conversation better. I'm glad I have friends in my life willing to be honest about how they feel, but I also think they could've handled bringing those concerns to me. They ganged up on me and made it seem like my feelings don't matter. I know that wasn't what they intended, and just want the best for me, but that doesn't make it hurt any less.

I finally make it back to our Airbnb after a pretty

refreshing walk. I'm glad I didn't end up calling an Uber; the walk helped me clear my head a bit.

Once I'm inside, I immediately change into comfy clothes and make myself a cup of tea. I settle into bed and take a couple of deep breaths to orient myself, willing my body to freaking *relax*. I'm tense from tonight, but also from the mounting stress of this…whatever this thing is with Jack.

I'm in new territory here. Not only have I never been in love before, but I've never fallen in love with a guy who lives halfway across the world from me. I don't doubt that long-distance relationships work. I've had several friends who've executed long-distance relationships successfully. They were miserable, but they did it.

I could do long-distance. We can probably make this work, I think to myself.

My hopeful thoughts are quickly squashed by their negative counterparts.

It's too far. There's no way this is sustainable long term.

I sink into the pillow a little further, doubt and dread keeping me company as I try to untangle the mess that is my thoughts.

My phone vibrates, and I feel lighter simply reading the name that pops up on my screen.

Jack: Missed you today, Kaia girl. Hope you had a great day.

Me: I missed you, too. So much. Dinner was okay! How was your day? Everyone survive the whole jumping-out-of-a-plane thing?

Jack: Is everything okay? With dinner, I mean.

He knows me so well already.

Me: Oh, yeah! All good.

I wouldn't even know where to start, so I make a mental note to fill him in later.

I add, Don't deflect from giving me the skydiving recap, Evil Canevil. Who broke a bone? Was it Angus? Please tell me you still have all of your fingers.

He responds with a laughing emoji followed by, All bones are intact and fingers attached. It was really fun! I was much more scared than I expected to be once I got up there, and I screamed the whole way down. But lots of fun was had overall, especially by Lachlan. I think he cried from sheer joy.

Me: He cried? That's really sweet. Good, I'm really glad you had fun. And that you kept all your fingers.

Jack: I'm excited to see you tomorrow. Can't wait to kiss that sweet face of yours. I've been thinking about it all day. What have you done to me? He says with a winky face.

Me: HAHAHA, my evil plan is working! Make you fall in love with me and buy me gelato for the rest of my life.

Jack: Lol, I'll do anything if it means I get to see you every day for the rest of my life.

I pause for a minute, staring at his message, tears forming behind my eyes. Why can't I connect the dots between what I want and what I feel is possible with this relationship? I want that. I want Jack and everything that comes along with having him for the rest of my life.

Can't wait to see you tomorrow, I type,

wiping away the tears that had fallen.

Jack: I love you. I'm counting down the hours, he says with a heart emoji.

I move to put my phone down but it buzzes again.

Jack: Also, I know we have talked a lot about me leaving and what that looks like, but we can talk all about it tomorrow. I just want you to know that I'm all in. I'm not going anywhere, not when it comes to us, at least. I'm confident in this, in us. Good night, Kaia girl.

CHAPTER 21: KAIA

Am I exaggerating when I say that kissing Jack is one of the best things I've ever done in my life? You might think so, but honestly, I'm not. Even the short, sweet kisses are beyond anything I ever dreamed or imagined kissing someone could be. It feels different than anything I've experienced before, an *electric* kind of different.

Jack and I are sitting inside a gelato shop, eating our favorite flavors, making googly eyes at each other across the table, and kissing in between spoonfuls like a couple of lovesick teenagers. It took twice as long as it normally would for us to walk here because we stopped every couple of yards, literally unable to keep our hands to ourselves. I've never felt anything like the joy and safety I feel when I'm with him.

And the comfort of his presence is exactly what I need after last night—even if my conflicting emotions about our relationship are sort of why I need comforting in the first place.

I didn't tell him about the fight with the girls. I feel like I'm still in the thick of sorting everything out, and I don't want to haul him into the mess with me. Once I figure it all out, I'll present it to him in a nice, neat package.

A girl can dream, right?

Instead, I focus on what's right in front of me. Jack loves me. He's right here, right now, and he *loves* me. I know this revelation happened only days ago, and even though we've been inseparable since, I really did not see this coming. I think my lack of being able to prepare for something like this only fuels my anxiety about whether or not we are setting ourselves up for heartbreak. Are three days of pure perfection worth whatever hardships long distance brings?

"I reckon you're in your head right now, aren't ya?" Jack says, breaking me from my train of thought, his hand making small, dizzying circles along my back.

"That obvious?" I say with a sheepish grin, taking

another small spoonful of the chocolate gelato in front of me.

I think my brain might need an entire month to process and come to terms with everything that's happened during my time in Paris so far.

"I've dreamt about this," Jack says as he scoots his chair closer to mine. Then he sets his warm hands on me, one cupping my face, the other strong on the back of my neck, pulling me closer. When we're a breath away, he leans in for a kiss.

"For the record, it's better than my dreams," he says against my lips. "So much better."

Jack pulls back, and his gaze goes hazy, the corner of his mouth tilting up like he knows exactly what I'm thinking about. Blushing, I smile and look down at the table for a beat before returning his gaze.

"Tell me what you're thinking," he challenges, and my blush deepens.

"Oh," I say with the spoon still in my mouth, "absolutely nothing at all, why do you ask?" I try for alluring and mysterious, but I have no poker face.

Jack laughs, then he reaches out and grabs my hand, entwining our fingers. "Thank you, Kaia."

"For gelato?" I ask, my eyebrows drawing together

in confusion.

"Sure," he chuckles. "And, I don't know, just for being you." He squeezes my hand softly, a gesture that shouldn't feel as intimate as it does. "For making me incredibly happy." Another squeeze. "For being willing to tell me how you feel." *Squeeze.* "and for being such a great human. Meeting you has been the best and most unexpected part of this trip, and my life will never be the same because of it. And I don't want it to be."

With his words, my heart swells. He's so sweet and thoughtful, and his love for me is palpable. Which is why I'm so frustrated by the sadness slowly expanding in my chest, tainting the joy, the comfort, and the hope I feel when I'm with Jack. I can't quiet the cacophony of negative feelings echoing in the back of my mind, taking over what should be a beautiful moment with him.

Jack reaches over and gently tilts my chin up to meet his eyes. "What's going through your head, Kai?"

Everything. Every emotion that I could possibly feel and every thought I could possibly have…I feel them in every fiber of my being.

"I'm not a hundred percent sure if I'm being honest." It's a lie, but it's also not.

He moves his thumb back and forth along my jaw, sending a jolt of electricity through my entire body.

The way I feel when this man touches me is not normal.

He leans forward, planting a soft, sweet kiss on my lips. "I'm here, Kaia."

He loves me, which steadies me, but also spins me out of control at the same time. And I love him—I've loved him for a while now, and I should be grateful to have found him, despite how unconventional this situation may be. This is the best-case scenario—the moment I've thought about since we met. This is everything I could ask for, and more.

But the sense of dread taking root in my heart begins to grow, and I can no longer pretend it doesn't exist. It's becoming all-consuming.

I quickly pull back from Jack with a soft smile. "Is it hot in here? I feel like I'm sweating a lot. Are you sweating?"

Confusion flashes across his face. Of course, he's confused as to why I'm suddenly acting like a crazy person.

I'm confused, too, buddy. Don't worry.

"Uhh, I don't think so. Are you okay?" he asks, sounding equal parts confused and concerned.

"Who, me? Yeah! I'm so okay. I'm great." I shed the sweater I'm wearing in an unintentionally dramatic fashion and stand up from my seat. "I'm gonna grab some fresh air really quick. I'll, uh, be right back."

I get up and make a break for the door before I can catch his response. The moment I'm outside, the sounds of a Parisian evening circle me, but I can barely hear them over the sound of my runaway thoughts.

This will never work.

He's leaving tomorrow.

You live halfway across the world.

He only loves you because it's new and exciting.

Once the reality of everyday settles in, he'll change his mind—they always do.

Oh yeah, and you live halfway across the world.

I'm flooded with thoughts of why this is the worst idea ever, and I can't think straight. Practicality is comfortable for me, and this situation makes me feel the opposite of comfortable.

I'm out of control. I've lost control of my life and

I'm no longer thinking straight.

The thoughts continue, each one like a flashing neon sign in my mind, lighting up with each deep breath I take to attempt to calm myself down. They get louder and louder until it's all I can hear. The beating of my heart plays in my ears like it's filtering through a megaphone, and I feel like the world is moving at hyper-speed around me.

Suddenly, a hand gently grabs my wrist, grounding me, bringing me back to reality. I hadn't realized I'd begun pacing.

"Hey, hey, hey—what's happening, Kaia? Let me be here with you." Jack grips both of my arms as if he can tell I feel like I'm going to float away. That, or maybe I look as unsteady as I feel.

Warm hands cup my face, and the man I'm madly in love with is looking me directly in the eyes, concern written all over his face. I can feel how much he genuinely cares about me. I know because the feeling is mutual.

"Jack, I love you." The truth.

Hot tears build behind my eyes, and my lip quivers as I speak.

He smiles, lacing his fingers with mine. "I love—"

"But it's not gonna work," I cut him off with a sob and wiggle out of his grip.

My actions seem foreign to even me, but for some reason, I can't stop the downward spiral I'm in. I cross my arms and stare straight down at my feet.

"I don't understand. What happened?" Jack asks, every syllable wrapped in frustration and confusion. But I can tell he's trying to hold it together for me.

"Nothing, I'm just…thinking more clearly."

I can't even look him in the eye. I keep my gaze on my shoes, a pair of tan loafers once again being stained by tears.

These must be bad luck. I should throw these shoes out, I can't help but think as my apparent path toward self-sabotage continues.

"Kaia, I'm in love with you—nothing is more clear to me than that. I don't care that this has happened quickly, or that we live in two different countries. This is the dream. *You* are the dream. And I'm willing to do whatever it takes to make it work." He steps closer, gingerly, as if he's afraid he might spook me, and cups my cheeks in his hands, forcing my gaze up to his. "I mean it, I'm in this. I want you. We can figure it out. I want to figure this out together."

It's possibly the sweetest, most tender moment I've ever experienced, coupled with the declaration of love that I've only dreamed about since meeting him, and yet, my brain can't even fully comprehend everything he's offering me. I've already shut down out of pure self-preservation and panic. I'm in full self-destruction mode. I'm sinking and I'm taking Jack down with me. No life vest in sight.

I'm going to fall apart right here, I'm sure of it. I'm trying hard to maintain my composure, but it's cracking and fraying at the edges. "When I'm back home, I'll be going to bed at the same time you're getting up for the day. You'll be getting ready for a night on the town while I'll be making my morning coffee." Confusion crosses his face as he's realizing what I'm saying.

"Kaia." A promise and a warning, wrapped neatly in the two syllables of my name.

"There are countries and oceans between us. It doesn't make sense. Sure, we can travel back and forth —but for how long? Until one of us decides to pack up our whole life and move in with the other? Until we both resent each other?" I say through tears.

"Woah, woah, woah. Slow down, Kai—"

"No, you're not listening to me, Jack." My voice is louder than I mean for it to be, and I'm thankful there isn't anyone around to witness my breakdown right now.

I'm angry now. Not at him, but at time zones, and flight prices, and the universe…and myself, for the doubt and lies coming out of my mouth that are bound to hurt this man I'm absolutely head over heels for. "I just…can't do this, okay?" I say, emotionally drained already.

"You *can't* do this, or you *won't?*" he asks, his tone clipped.

I look up and make direct eye contact with him for the first time since this conversation started. He's hurt—anger, and disappointment evident in his beautiful features. The disappointment is a direct hit to my heart.

I did this.

And I want to take it all back.

I want to tell him that I love him, but I'm so scared. I want to tell him that he's the best thing that's ever happened to me, and I'm scared of losing him. I'm scared of this not working. I'm scared of years wasted, building resentment—a deeper hurt because of deeper love.

It hurts now, but nothing compared to what it could be after experiencing a full life with Jack.

"I won't," I say, understanding that those two words communicate the end of the conversation. The end of us.

He shakes his head slowly, reluctantly breaking his gaze from mine and looking off in another direction. "Okay."

"Okay," I say, my rasped voice sounding like it belongs to someone else.

A few moments of silence pass, and I realize I need to get out of here. Now.

"I'm gonna head back to my place," I say, quietly. I'm desperately holding back more tears, and I don't want him to see me cry anymore.

I feel his gaze on me, willing me to look at him and fight for this.

I don't. I can't, because I don't know how.

"Can I walk you?"

Even after ripping his heart out of his chest, he still offers to walk me home like the absolute gentleman that he is. I almost lose it right there.

I quickly wipe the oncoming tears away

"I'll call an Uber. It's quicker."

Out of the corner of my eye, I see him nod his head in understanding and shove his hands in his pockets.

God, he's handsome. I want to throw my arms around him and tell him that I didn't mean any of it, but I can't. Because a part of me does mean it. Or, at the very least, the fear behind this episode of self-sabotage is legitimate. The way I handled it, however?

Awful, I know.

I watch the man I love walk away from me, looking utterly heartbroken and defeated.

I open my phone and order an Uber. Once it's confirmed, I check for the next available flight to Seattle. I have to get out of this city before it breaks my heart any more than it already has.

CHAPTER 22: JACK

I won't.

I let the words reverberate in my mind, replaying the moment Kaia told me that she wouldn't do this—wouldn't do *us*. In that moment, I tried to keep it together as best as I could. I wanted to be calm for her because I think she's scared. Hell, I'm *terrified* of how strongly I care about her. I guess for this reason, exactly. Terrified of the possibility of getting my heart ripped out of my chest, left alone and heartbroken in front of a gelato shop in Paris. Terrified of losing her.

And I did.

I wanted to chase after her, to tell her that it's okay for her to be afraid. I wanted to fight for her. But that would've been selfish because I know that's not what she needs. She knows how I feel about her, at least I hope she does. I love her. And I guess that's why I let her go.

If this is what's best for her, then so be it. Even if it hurts like hell. Even if it feels like I have a Kaia-sized hole in my chest.

My feet are on autopilot as I walk away from the gelato shop, and I hope that I'm heading in the right direction of Lachlan's place. Paris nightlife bustles around me, but I don't really process any of it. I can't hear much over the faint ringing in my ears and the sound of Kaia's parting words replaying over and over again in my head.

I don't know how long I walk, but I eventually make it back to the house. I walk in and right past Lachlan and Angus sitting in the living room. At first glance, it looks like they're enjoying a drink and a round of cards, but I don't stop to inspect further, and I certainly don't stop to talk. I don't want to talk about it. I'm not ready to relive the heartbreak out loud. Not yet. Saying the words aloud will only make them real, and permanent.

"Hey, mate—you good?" Lachlan calls after me,

and I give him a quick thumbs up over my shoulder before heading into my room and shutting the door.

I look around the room and all I see are remnants of *her*, unable to escape the fracture in my heart that's growing by the second. On the floor next to the bed is the shirt I wore to Lachlan's birthday party, the same one I was wearing when I told Kaia I love her for the first time. The one I was wearing when I got to truly hold her for the first time. I remember thinking that it had been so long since I felt *at home* with another person like I do with Kaia. Or *did*. And I wonder how I'm supposed to go on feeling at home somewhere else now knowing that I said goodbye to it less than an hour ago.

I see a napkin rose on the nightstand—one I made the night we all went to the fondue restaurant and I needed something to do with my hands while Lachlan flirted with the girl I was secretly crazy about. I tucked my hands under the table and fidgeted with my napkin until I formed a rose—something I do often. I quickly tucked it into my pocket and planned to throw it away, but for some reason, I couldn't. I held onto it because it reminded me of Kaia. And it still does.

A knock on the door jolts me back to reality, and I stand up fully from where I was leaning back against the door.

"I won't ask, but we're here if you want to talk, mate," Angus says from the other side of the door, his voice empathetic.

Before I can respond, Lachlan chimes in, and it sounds like he has his mouth literally pressed to the crack between the wall and the door. If I wasn't so numb right now, that might've made me laugh. "Left you an Old Fashioned by the door. I hear it cures a broken heart…or…whatever you're going through."

They know it has to do with Kaia because of course they do.

I don't respond initially, but I know they're lingering and figure I should at least give them something.

"Thank you. I appreciate you, mates."

"Jack, if you want to talk about it now, I'll order us some pizzas, and we—" Lachlan starts but is quickly cut off by Angus shushing him, and soon, their footsteps retreat down the hall toward the living room.

"Whenever you're ready, brother!" Angus yells in

what I guess is a last-ditch effort to get me to talk about it.

I take a deep breath and open the door, only wide enough to tell if there's actually a drink out there or if Lachlan was trying to lure me out.

Sure enough, there's a drink sitting right outside my bedroom door. The caramel-colored liquid hits the glass at the halfway mark, the quintessential Old Fashioned orange peel resting right on top.

I grab it and shut the door quietly, once again leaning back on it.

I close my eyes and bring the glass up to my closed mouth, clenching my jaw so hard it hurts as I let the reality of tonight hit me, frustration settling into my bones.

I'm not frustrated with Kaia, though.

I'm frustrated with fear. Doubt. Uncertainty. All of the insidious things that try to convince us that something good in our lives, great even, won't work before we've even tried it. It happens to everyone.

And it's my hunch that's what happened here. But I can't do anything about it.

So, for right now, I'll drink an Old Fashioned. Tomorrow, I'll attempt to collect the pieces of my broken heart, shove them into my suitcase and head back to Australia, as if my life hasn't been forever changed by the last few weeks.

CHAPTER 23: KAIA

The Uber drops me off at our Airbnb about twenty-five minutes after my fight with Jack, if you can even call it that. It was more like me ripping Jack's heart out and stomping on it over and over again. At least that's what I feel like I did.

I slowly make my way up the spiral staircase to our flat, mentally preparing myself to explain to the girls what happened and that I'm leaving. Who am I kidding? Nothing can prepare me for that and, to be honest, all I want is to pack my bags and slip out without anyone noticing.

I open the front door and find Havannah sitting at the small dining room table with a cup of tea. She looks up at me, and her expression morphs into concern.

"Hey, Kai—you ok?" she asks. She doesn't get up. I imagine she's still upset about our conversation earlier. It's sweet of her to ask, but I don't feel like talking about it right now. I wouldn't know where to start, and having that conversation forces me to be more honest than I'm ready to be right now.

"Yeah, I'm ok. Or at least, I will be," I say, looking down at my hands, fiddling with the keys to our place. "I came to let you guys know that I booked a red-eye home. I'm going to pack my bags and head to the airport."

She doesn't look surprised. She does look sad, though, and I hate that. I don't want to hurt anyone, but I seem to be doing that a lot tonight.

"Ok. Callie and Adelina are asleep, but I can let them know tomorrow morning," she says quietly.

"Thank you. I really appreciate it," I say as I head toward my room.

"Do you need help packing?" she asks as I round the corner, and I could cry at her kind gesture, but I think I'm fresh out of tears for the night. It feels easier to do it myself and slip out. Or maybe it only feels more comfortable. To retreat. To hide. To avoid.

It's what I'm best at.

"That's ok. You enjoy the rest of your night and trip," I say and turn back quickly, heading into my room and quietly shutting the door. Once inside, I let the tears I'd been holding back since the Uber ride fall recklessly down my face. I cover my face with my hand to muffle the sounds of my sobbing as I release all the feelings that have been mounting since the moment I ruined probably one of the best things that have ever happened to me. For only a moment, I allow myself to fall apart.

"Peanuts or pretzels?"

The question snaps me out of my daze, and I look up at a semi-concerned flight attendant holding a bag of pretzels and a bag of peanuts in my direction. *Did she ask me that more than once?* I wonder.

"Uh…pretzels, thank you," I say in response and take the pretzels from her, which, from the feel of them, I can tell are crushed into tiny pieces.

I thought for sure I'd be relieved to be on my way home, but I'm not. Honestly, I feel worse than I did before I left, but I'm sure I'll feel better once I'm settled back into a routine at home.

The girls tried to convince me to stay, but I had already booked my flight home in the Uber after my excruciating talk with Jack, and my mind was made up. I needed to get home and back to real life—back to practical Kaia.

I spend a good portion of the flight catching up on as much sleep as I can, but I'm not very successful. Sleep has been difficult the past few days; I can't seem to turn my brain off. I keep replaying that conversation with Jack on a loop, the image of the devastation on his face seared into my mind.

When I'm not sleeping, I'm working on my resume and sending it out to some contacts I made in the industry and applying for jobs online. It's time to get back to it. I had my fun, but I need a job.

Opening my phone to update the running note of industry contacts to reach out to, my eye catches on my background. It's a picture of all seven of us—the girls, Jack, Lachlan, and Angus, posing for a very squished selfie along the Seine during a night out. We'd just had an amazing Italian dinner and decided to take the long route home to do some extra sightseeing.

We were singing and dancing in the street and overall acting like crazy people having the best night of their lives. And I think it might've been one of the best nights of mine. I felt so carefree and confident. I felt fully myself, surrounded by people who appreciated that about me. *I miss that.*

I quickly find my notes app and focus on what I originally grabbed my phone for in the first place, while simultaneously pushing all of those feelings aside and packing them in a small box in the corner of my brain labeled "for later."

I came home for a reason, and I need to focus on that.

"Welcome to Seattle! Enjoy your stay, and thank you for flying with us," is the first thing I hear as a bumpy landing jolts me awake. I finally fell asleep for a bit toward the end of the flight, and I forgot where I was for a minute.

I slowly pat my upper extremities to reorient myself and remind myself that I am alive and didn't die a tragic death in a fiery plane crash.

I must've been more outwardly startled than I

realize because the elderly man sitting next to me leans over and says, "You alright there, kid?"

He's about the same age as my grandpa, and he's wearing the sweetest sweatshirt. It has a childlike drawing of a fish with corresponding text that says "My Grandson is an Artist!" on the front. I don't know anything about this man, but from that alone, I get the feeling he's a pretty great human being.

I laugh. "Yeah, I'm okay. Just scared me a little. Thank you for checking."

He nods and goes back to reading his newspaper for a minute. He interrupts his reading not too long after and leans over again.

"I don't mean to pry, but what's a young gal like you doing looking so sad?"

It's really sweet of him to ask, but I honestly don't even know how to answer that.

"Oh you know…just feeling a little lost right now, that's all," I say with a quick grin. "I have a plan though—it'll all work out."

He smiles and places his warm hand over mine. I probably should be more weirded out by this stranger touching me, but I'm not. We'll call him my airplane grandpa—and I have a feeling he's exactly the wise voice I need in my life right now.

"You know, you don't always need a plan. Sometimes life is all about figuring it out as you go."

Wise, indeed, but I'm not so sure I believe him. How do you not have a plan? If I didn't plan, my life would implode or spontaneously combust. I smile and gather my things as we begin to exit the plane.

"Thank you so much. I appreciate your encouragement. I need all the encouragement I can get these days," I say and stick my hand out to shake his. "I'm Kaia, by the way."

"Well, I hope you find your way, and find what you're looking for. There's a lot of life to live out there for a young gal like yourself. Don't let it pass you by, ok?" He reaches out and takes my hand. "My name is Jack."

I stood there, still holding onto his hand, unable to move. Of course, my guardian angel slash wise airplane grandpa's name is Jack.

This is not a sign. This means nothing. It's just a coincidence, I think to myself as I return to reality and give this poor man his hand back.

I smile and give him an embarrassed chuckle then quickly make my way off the plane before I make a bigger fool out of myself than I already have.

The Uber home is quiet. I used to appreciate the quiet more than I currently do. Now, it leaves too much space for the many thoughts running through my head at all times. Most of them are about Jack.

It happened. It's over. I just need to move on, I think to myself.

This will be easy. I'm going to get home, settle in, sleep in my own bed, and things will start to look up. I'm sure of it.

CHAPTER 24: KAIA

I'm not going to lie, my first day home has been one of the worst days I've had in a while. I don't feel better at all. Not one bit. Not even close. I feel *worse* and more out of control than I did before I left Paris. I thought coming home would steady me, and center me, but instead, I feel like a stranger in my own bed. Like my bed isn't *my* bed. My apartment feels foreign. It's odd and sort of depressing.

Not to mention…I have no job, no relationship with the man I'm in love with, and I'm pretty sure my friends hate me right now. Ok, I know they don't *hate* me…but I don't think I'm their favorite person.

"Hello! Can someone let me in?" I shout through the thick door outside my parent's house after taking a deep breath and trying to clear my head of the why-don't-I-feel-back-to-normal-yet pity party I've been throwing ever since landing back on U.S. soil.

"I've had this key for like fifteen years—why is it not working?" I say to myself and try again. No luck. I knock again, slightly more aggressive this time.

My family and I try to have dinner every couple of weeks. My sister is in Atlanta on a work trip and my brother won an all-expense paid trip to Cabo on the radio. I'm the only Griffen kid here, and somehow I forgot how to unlock a door. Should I add this to the list of things I left behind in Paris? The ability to unlock doors?

Either that, or they changed the lock and forgot to tell me.

It's freezing outside, and I'm probably going to be eaten by a bear or something if I'm out here for much longer.

Finally, footsteps and muffled voices head toward the door, so I take a step back and wait for my rescuer.

"Hi, sweetie!" My dad opens the door, and a confused look comes over his face. "Wait, why didn't you use your key?"

"Hey, Dad!" I lean in to hug him. "I tried to use my key, but it didn't work."

"Honey, we changed the lock, remember?" I hear my mom shout from the other room.

"OH! Right, we did. Sorry about that, pumpkin. You weren't out there long, were you?"

"Only long enough to get frostbite on two of my toes, so I think I'll live."

"Oh good, good. At least you'll get to keep all your fingers—those are useful for all that texting you do," he says with a laugh.

My dad and I have always had a fun, back-and-forth banter. It's gentle enough that we're not hurting each other's feelings but pointed enough that onlookers who don't know us might actually think we're fighting.

"Kaia, honey—how are you?" My mom greets me with a hug while holding a giant ladle covered in tomato sauce. I hug her back and try to strategically avoid ending up with a giant red stain on my shirt.

My mom is the chef of the family, and I swear she always has some type of cooking utensil in her hands at all times. She loves it. She says it's her version of therapy. Although she goes to real therapy, too, so I guess she's probably the most stable one out of the five of us Griffens.

"I'm making my classic spaghetti and meatballs for dinner. I hope that's okay," my mom says, pulling back from the hug with a smile.

"That's perfect, Mom. Thank you," I reply.

"Why'd you guys change the lock, anyway?"

"Oh, that reminds me! Here's your new key, honey." My mom reaches into the junk drawer, pulls out a shiny new key, and hands it to me.

"I'll let your dad tell you the lock story," Mom says as she and my dad exchange a few funny looks I can't quite decipher, but the story involves some sort of disagreement that my mom clearly won.

My dad takes a deep breath and lets out a quick laugh. "Look, it was bright and early in the morning and I hadn't had my coffee yet."

My mom lets out an exasperated, "Mhm," under her breath while she stirs her sauce. This is better than reality TV, honestly.

"*Mhm*, yeah. Anyway, I hadn't had my coffee yet, and I went down the block to get the mail and didn't realize I had locked the door on my way out. I usually keep it unlocked when I run down the street."

"Right," I add, to let my dad know I'm keyed in and very interested in his story. I usually do this because it helps him around the corner to his points faster. He's quite a talker, but we love it.

"So I don't normally lock the door, and I guess I did by accident, but like I said… hadn't had coffee yet and my brain wasn't turned on."

This is absolutely where I get my coffee addiction from. Neither my dad nor I are functioning human beings before our morning cups. So I get it.

"So, I may or may not have tried to unlock the door with the mail key that was in my hand and… I, er, may or may not have broken the mailbox key off in the lock on the front door."

My mom swings around once again with the sauce-covered spoon in her hand, flinging some sauce onto the counter next to her. She has a smile on her face, and it looks like she's trying not to laugh.

"Here I was, trying to enjoy my cup of coffee and my morning read, and I hear this awful noise coming from the front door. I thought someone was trying to break in for a minute until I peeked around the corner and saw your dad through the window," she says.

My dad jumps in. "And she comes barreling out

the door faster than a cheetah! You would've thought Macy's had announced a ninety-five percent off sale, and she was on her way to the mall to spend all of our money."

"Oh, hush!" My mom throws a pot holder in my dad's direction, laughing as she does it.

"You guys are crazy," I say with a laugh.

We had a delicious pasta dinner thanks to my mom, and it was dinner and a show thanks to the witty humor and banter from my dad. I love coming to my parent's house. It's always so low-key and light-hearted.

We're not a perfect family by any means. We all have our stuff, and we've had some tough seasons, but mostly, my parents really are laid back. When I was younger, sometimes that bothered me, but not so much anymore. I used to worry that because they were so chill about everything, it meant that they didn't care, but now I know that's not the case. Now, I know it's because they trust me.

We've settled into the living room with hot chocolate in various ornate and over-the-top

Christmas mugs my mom likes to use all year round.

I'm lucky enough to get to use the reindeer mug… and I'm not talking about a mug shaped like a cute reindeer face. This mug is the shape of a full reindeer —head, body, arms, and legs. It's incredibly detailed too, with brush strokes imitating the fur and clear irises in the eyes. It's my least favorite of the mugs in my mom's Christmas collection because it creeps me out, but I always end up with it, and my mom loves it. So, I can pretend to love it, too.

I feel my mom looking at me, so I turn to face her and find her expression is one I'm all too familiar with. She knows I'm sad, and wants to fix it, but she knows she can't, so she looks at me with her big, blue puppy dog eyes, willing me to no longer be heartbroken because she hates to see me sad.

"I hate to see you sad, sweetie."

Called it.

"I know, Mom. I'll be okay, just gotta give it time to blow over." I look up and give her my best I'm-a-brave-girl smile, and she gives me a softer one in return.

"You really love him, don't you?" my dad says from his recliner.

I look down at my hot chocolate mug, absentmindedly swirling the stirring spoon around in circles.

An image of Jack's smile pops into my head, and the pang of sorrow that follows makes me wince.

I close my eyes and take a deep breath, letting it out slow and steady, focusing on my breath and not the tears stinging the back of my eyes. "Yeah, I do."

My parents don't push the subject. They just sit with me and let me silently process, my mom occasionally putting her hand on my knee or my shoulder to comfort me.

"Here for you, Kaia. Always." My mom says.

CHAPTER 25: KAIA

It's ten a.m., and I can't bring myself to get out of bed. Not because I'm comfy, but because I don't want to face the day. If I stay here, the reality of the mess that is my life simply doesn't exist.

Except it does…because I have a job interview in two hours. One that I should probably be excited for. I was sort of excited when I applied, but I was overcome immediately with a sense of dread once I got the email about scheduling an interview.

I wonder if I'm sentencing myself to another six years at a job that I'll hate while my dreams float further and further down the proverbial river that is life.

Who knows. I don't have the option to worry

about that right now because this job will pay the bills, and right now, that's all I need to care about.

I slouch my body over the edge of the bed and, very dramatically, drag myself up and out until I'm standing. I rub my eyes, take a good stretch, and head to my closet to grab the same outfit I wear to every interview. It's my quintessential job interview outfit, and it makes me feel pretty darn professional.

I pull my hair back into a low, uniform bun and put on some minimal makeup before making a cup of coffee.

Please make me act and feel more like a functioning human being, I silently chant into my coffee, willing it to bring me back to life.

I grab my keys and head to my car, where I play the Taylor Swift Essentials playlist. I figured a T-Swift car dance party might pump me up, and I was not wrong. I'm sure the cars next to me on the highway enjoyed the show as well.

I pull into the parking garage of a rather fancy office building and smooth out any wrinkles in my blazer before heading in.

Once inside, I admire the ginormous crystal chandelier in the foyer. I'm no expert on light fixtures, but if I had to guess, I would say it's worth more than my life's savings…times ten.

The receptionist at the front desk looks up at me with a cheery smile, and it's exactly the warm welcome I need to calm my nerves. *Maybe I would like it here,* I think.

"Hi, miss! How can I help you?" she asks politely.

"I'm here for an interview with Mr—"

She stops me before I can finish.

"Oh, you're Ms. Griffen! Yes, of course. He's excited to meet you. I'll let him know you're here."

"Thanks so much," I say with a smile.

Well, that sure is a boost of confidence.

I walk over to check out the art they have at the opposite end of the foyer. It looks like a community art display, done by kids from a nearby school for the deaf, and this firm sponsors their yearly fundraising event. The art is really beautiful, and I love that they've chosen to showcase it here at their office.

"We're ready for you!" the receptionist says from her desk.

I quickly smooth my blazer with my hands one last time and take a deep breath before heading over.

As soon as I walk into the conference room, a tall

man in a suit stands and motions to give me a handshake. "Hi, Ms. Griffen, my name is Michael Lyle. I'm the managing partner here. It's a pleasure to meet you," he says with a kind smile.

"Nice to meet you, Mr. Lyle. I appreciate you taking the time to meet with me."

He gestures for me to have a seat and asks if I'd like any water.

"Water would be great. Thank you so much."

Once settled with my water, he dives right into the interview questions. I'm not nervous anymore, which I'm thankful for. I feel like I can answer questions more effectively when I'm not as nervous.

The interview itself is pretty low-key. Straightforward questions, and I don't feel like I have to work hard to impress with my answers. I feel like I can be myself here, and that's a bright green flag if you ask me. I'm thinking it could really work out here if I ended up getting this job.

"We're coming up on our hour meeting time here, so I won't take up too much more of your time. I just have one additional question, but it's more of a fun one," he says with a smile.

"Ok, go for it!" I say.

"Where do you see yourself in five years, Ms. Griffen?"

When Mr. Lyle clears his throat, I realize I've been silent for too long.

"I'm sorry, what did you say?" I ask, probably more intensely than I meant to.

He looks confused. "I, uh…I asked you where you see yourself in five years?"

"Okay, yes, right. I'm sorry. That question just caught me off guard," I confess, feeling flustered. I readjust my position in the chair and ponder the thought.

"Where do I see myself in five years?" I repeat under my breath, staring at the landscape painting on the wall behind Mr. Lyle, who is probably questioning whether or not I'm having a stroke and need medical intervention.

Where do I see myself in five years?

I want to be able to say that question would require some introspection, and that I would come back to it, but in reality?

It's easy to picture where I want to be in five years. I want to be a practicing lawyer, helping as many people as I can—doing meaningful work. But it's more than that. I want to run my own firm. If I'm honest with myself, that's always been my dream. It's what I based my law school personal statement on when I applied to schools.

Why was I so quick to abandon that goal?

And let's be honest, in five years, I see Jack and I cuddled on a couch in a beautiful cozy living room in a home that we created together. We're eating popcorn and watching reruns of *New Girl*, taking turns quoting Schmidt. We're together, and it feels right. It's always felt right.

In five years…I don't picture myself at this job. Not one bit.

What am I doing here?

"Excuse me?" Mr. Lyle asks, confusion and surprise etched on his face.

Oh no. I definitely did not think that to myself. I said that out loud.

"I'm so sorry, forgive me." I stand and smooth my hands down the perfectly ironed slacks I have on. The ones that I don't like that much, but I keep for occasions such as this one—job interviews for positions that I undoubtedly will hate but pay the bills. My practical pants, if you will.

I look Mr. Lyle directly in the eye and extend my hand forward.

He shakes my hand, looking very confused. "I'm not sure what's happening here."

That makes two of us.

"I think I'm having a moment. Maybe a slight identity crisis." Great, okay, now we're oversharing. And I'm still shaking his hand. I quickly let go and shoulder my purse.

"I appreciate you taking the time to meet with me. I just don't think this is right for me," I say, adding, "I'm sorry to have wasted your time."

He looks up at me, face shifting with empathy and maybe a little bit of sadness. Almost like he understands what I'm experiencing, as if he's felt it before, too.

"It was no time wasted. A pleasure to meet you, Ms. Griffen." I'm about to walk out of the office when he adds, "I hope you find what you're looking for.

I pause, feeling deep in my bones that I've already found what I'm looking for, I was just too scared to hold on to it.

"Thank you, Mr. Lyle. Me, too."

My subconscious walks me out to my car, my heart pounding and my mind buzzing, replaying the events of the last few months of my life.

I'm realizing probably what everyone has been trying to tell me all along.

I've been letting my life just happen to me like I'm a passenger watching my life go by in the rearview mirror.

I've stayed in places that didn't serve me simply because I thought it was the practical thing to do… and because starting over sounded too scary. I resisted change and risk at nearly every turn. And more than that, I think I resisted every opportunity for true happiness—a fullness of life that I have been craving for years.

I yank the rearview mirror toward me and make eye contact with a girl I hardly recognize anymore. A girl who fights with her best friends for being brutally honest with her, a girl who stays in a toxic work environment out of complacency, and a girl who leaves love behind out of fear.

"Who are you?" I ask the girl in the mirror.

I exhale deeply, forgiving myself for being so blind while I held onto my ten-year plan for dear life, truly believing that nothing could possibly go wrong if I simply stuck to that plan. And while that offered a sense of security, it stifled opportunities for good things, too. Things I was meant for.

My mind flashes to a rainstorm in Paris, stuck under an awning, the chill from the rain nothing compared to the thrill of the closeness to Jack.

First things first, I need to be honest about what I want to do with my life, and I think that's finally admitting to myself that I want to start my own firm.

And while that is a terrifying thought, it's also so liberating.

Second, I need to tell a very handsome Australian man that I made a mistake and hope that he forgives me.

CHAPTER 26: KAIA

"Mocha for Kaia!"

I get up from the cafe table to grab my coffee from the bar at the cute little coffee shop around the corner from my house, which I don't come to often enough.

I sit down and smile at my table mate, full of gratitude that this meeting happened on such short notice.

"Thanks so much for meeting me, Layla. I really needed this."

"Are you kidding me? I'm here whenever you need me—plus, it's good to see you. I haven't seen you since that firm made, in my opinion, the dumb decision to let you go."

I blush at the compliment.

Hadley and Scott letting me go certainly threw a wrench in things, but it also may have been the best thing to ever happen to me.

"You look good, though," she adds. "How are you?"

"I'm good…" I say, testing the word and finding it's the truth. "I'm okay. I'm getting there, I think."

"Good. Any job prospects?"

"Actually, that's why I asked you to meet me here." I smile at her sheepishly. I'm not sure why I'm so nervous about telling her my idea, but it's sort of eating me up inside.

She smiles. "I'm listening."

"Well, basically ever since I knew I wanted to be an attorney, I've wanted to open my own firm. And I wanted a large portion of our operations to be pro bono work. So…sort of like a nonprofit law firm." I pause for interjections but continue when she gestures for me to keep going.

"I guess it just felt like too big of a dream at the time, or maybe I just felt like I needed more corporate experience under my belt, so I never pursued it. From there, after getting my job at the firm, I just got sucked in. I started doing work I didn't want to do because I wanted to be helpful, not to mention it put me on the fast track to becoming a partner, which I hadn't anticipated…and I lost sight of what I wanted to accomplish in my career."

I take a sip of my coffee and continue, gaining confidence in my vision for the future with every word I speak.

"I had a job interview last week with a great firm. Full benefits, amazing pay, and a corner office with a view. And once I got in there, I just…couldn't deny the feeling of knowing that was not the direction I'm supposed to go right now. All I felt was a disconnect, and I couldn't have moved forward with it even if I wanted to. I was going to call you right then and there and ask if I was having a stroke or something."

Layla laughs, but still stays quiet, letting me get out all of my thoughts, as disorganized as they may be. I press on after another sip of my coffee, letting the warmth spread through me as I share my dream with my coworker turned mentor turned friend.

"I slept on it, and that night, I had a dream about opening my own firm. It was so vivid I thought for sure it was real. I saw the number of people we helped in one day of business, and even though it was a dream, I can't stop thinking about what an impact it could have on the community."

I swipe at a quick tear that had fallen without me realizing it. "I think this could work, and I think it could be amazing for those who need it."

I look up and realize Layla had started crying as well. She reaches across the table and grabs my hand in hers. "Kaia, I feel like I've been waiting for you to realize what you're capable of since the moment I met you."

Cue additional tears.

"Not only is this an amazing idea, but I know you can do it. And I know it's going to be life-changing for so many people, our community, and beyond."

She squeezes my hand and pulls hers back to her coffee cup. "If you're looking for my endorsement, you've got it. And if you need anything else from me, you can count on it. I'm on your side, and I believe in you wholeheartedly."

I wipe the many tears that have fallen now since Layla started talking. I should've known I was going to cry—she's got a way with words.

"Thank you so much, Layla. Truly, all of that

means so much."

CHAPTER 27: KAIA

"These aren't spirit fingers, *these* are spirit fingers!" I hear from the living room as I pour the slightly burnt popcorn into a bowl. I accidentally burnt the popcorn, but…I secretly prefer it burnt.

This is our first girl's night since Paris, and I'm so excited to get together with the girls again. I've done quite a bit of reflecting since the trip, including replaying that night in the pizza shop over and over again, wishing I had handled things differently. Or at least expressed myself better in the moment.

That seems to be a theme when reflecting on my last few hours in Paris.

Once I got home, not even an entire twenty-four hours went by before I called the girls on a group

FaceTime call to apologize for the way it all went down. It turned into a two-hour-long bestie therapy session, and we were all crying ugly, happy tears by the end.

I walk into the living room, and Callie throws a pillow in my direction. I make a dramatic move of dodging it and act as if I barely escaped with my life.

"You think you're so sneaky! You totally burnt the popcorn on purpose!" she jokes.

"I can neither confirm nor deny, but I will remind you that I'm innocent until proven guilty." I laugh and set the popcorn on the coffee table, next to the sour straws and Milky Way Midnights.

Havannah yelps with excitement at the Milky Way Midnights—they're her favorite, even though I'd never even heard of them until she mentioned that. Now, every time we have them, she'll make me eat one and convince me that they're the best candy on the planet. They're not my favorite—I actually can't stand Milky Ways—but I eat one every time and pretend that they're growing on me because she still gets this hopeful look on her face like I'm going to come to my senses and admit I love them.

"You know the drill. Here, Kaia!" She tosses me

one and watches adamantly for me to eat it.

I laugh. "Okay, okay. Can you not stare at me like a crazy person?"

I open the small square of chocolate that I loathe and pop it into my mouth. I raise my eyebrows in surprise and say, "Wait, this is a pretty good batch. This might be the one I've liked the most."

"See! I told you. I knew you'd like them eventually," she exclaims, and we all laugh.

"So, Kai. How've you been?" Adelina asks. I guess we're getting right to the nitty gritty.

"I'm good," I say, and she immediately gives me a skeptical look.

"No, really. I'm actually good. I've had a ton of time to think lately, and I'm confident with where it's brought me."

The girls lean in like I'm telling the most intriguing story that's ever been told.

I go on to tell them pretty much everything that's happened since I left Paris. I tell them how I expected to feel so much better—like myself again—when I got home. But all I did was find out that I never felt more like myself than I did when I was in Paris, living life to the fullest, not worrying about controlling every single aspect of my life.

I tell them about the job interview and my meeting with Layla. I tell them my plans of starting my own law firm—one that supports local charities and offers pro bono work for those who need it most. My voice shakes at this part because I'm so passionate about it, and finally putting into words this vision, this dream, that's been sitting dormant in my heart for so long feels like a puzzle piece clicking into place.

And lastly, I tell them about my feelings toward Jack, not that they weren't already wildly aware that I'm crazy about him. I tell them that I plan to apologize to him and see where it goes from there. I'm not expecting anything, and honestly, I'm keeping my hopes low to soften the blow of what might happen. All I know is that he deserves an apology from me.

I realize I actually am crying by the end of telling the girls my whole life story post-Paris, and Adelina leans in to hug me. She's crying, too, and before I know it, Havannah and Callie have joined in on the hug. We're all laughing through tears, savoring the group hug, and subsequently, this incredible friendship we've been blessed with.

CHAPTER 28: KAIA

I've been trying to distract myself by digging into a current NYT bestseller, but I've read the same sentence probably seven times, and I'm still not absorbing it. I'm saved from an eighth attempt by my phone buzzing on my bedside table. I set down my book, opened and turned over on my knees, as I reach for my phone. The screen lights up with a text from Lachlan.

Trust me, no one is more surprised than me by this turn of events. I had been thinking of texting him all week last week, but I couldn't muster up the courage to do so. We hadn't talked since I left Paris, and things between us felt awkward and unfinished. I kept typing out a message and quickly deleting it.

On Saturday, I finally sent the first message—then promptly threw my phone across the room—equal parts anxious and relieved knowing it couldn't be undone.

Of course, he responded right away, and I spent the next fifteen minutes trying to find my phone in a pile of throw pillows and blankets in my living room.

I pick up my phone and read the message I've been waiting for.

```
Lachlan: Jack's coming to Paris
again for a bit. Sort of licking his
wounds, you know?
```

I had reached out to Lachlan to see how Jack was doing.

I know, I know.

I could've reached out to Jack directly, but what I have to convey to him shouldn't be done over a text or even a lengthy phone call. I want to talk to him in person. I *need* to talk to him in person.

```
Me: How long is he there for?
```

I see the little bubble to signify Lachlan is typing and wait not-so-patiently for a response.

```
Lachlan: He heads back to Australia
next week.
```

I sit and think for a minute. My heart is pounding, and with absolute certainty and a whole lot of fear, I know exactly what it is I need to do.

I type with shaky hands.

Me: Okay, then I'm coming to Paris. This week.

"Hold on! You're going to Paris…tomorrow?" Callie shrieks from my computer, where I have her, Havannah, and Adelina on FaceTime.

I'm panic-packing for my flight, which leaves in approximately sixteen hours, digging through two different laundry baskets in an attempt to pack as quickly as possible. This is so unlike me, but I've never been so sure about something in my entire life. I'm a nervous wreck about taking a trip across the world on such short notice, but I know that Jack deserves to hear my apology in person. He also deserves to know how I feel, and why I panicked and fled from Paris in the first place.

I'm a nervous wreck about his reaction to me showing up unannounced. I don't blame him if he never wants to see me again, but that's a risk—and a chance for heartbreak—I'm willing to take.

"Please tell me you're bringing your black dress with the tiny, delicate flowers? You *have* to wear it when you see Jack again," Adelina says.

"Oh my God, *yes*! That one!" Havannah adds, pretending to drool.

I laugh and start rummaging through my closet for the dress in question. "Okay, okay! If I can find it in this mess I call a closet, I'll bring it."

"Okay, wait, tell me how this is all happening again?" Callie asks, obviously still not over the fact that this time tomorrow I'll be in Paris once again.

"Well, I wanted to, or more so *needed to,* apologize to Jack in person. So I reached out to Lachlan…"

I pause, noting their shocked expressions as Havannah shouts "*Lachlan?*"

"I know, I know!" I say, holding up my hands, a black dress with delicate flowers dangling from my fingers. I fold it and put it in my suitcase before I continue. "So I asked if he could sort of help me figure out how to visit Jack, and he agreed," I say like it's the simplest plan in the whole world.

Super easy. Piece of cake.

"So, wait…The guy who professed his love for you

while drunk at his birthday party is helping you re-profess your love to his best friend…who also is in love with you," Adelina says slowly.

It's silent for a moment before we all break into a laugh because, when you say it like that, it is quite ridiculous.

"Yep, basically—that's exactly it," I say, inhaling a shaky breath and looking at the screen with a small smile.

"For real though, Kai—how do you feel?" Callie asks.

"I feel like I'm going to poop my pants at any moment," I joke, but in a way that says I'm not at all joking. I do feel like that.

I start rolling up more clothes for my suitcase, not even looking at what I'm packing at this point.

"I'm also excited, though." I shrug. "I've thought about Jack practically *every* second since I left, and I need him to know how I feel about him," I say, stuffing more into my suitcase.

"Kaia—that was a kitchen towel," Lina points out.

I look down, realizing she's right. I laugh as I take it out of my suitcase and try to exhale. While I am really nervous, I'm also truly excited about seeing Jack again. Even if it's this one last time.

"Are you sure you don't need us to come over?" Havannah asks.

"It's really fine," I assure them. "I'm going to *try* and sleep for a few hours before heading to the airport obnoxiously early."

"Kaia, I am so proud of you for doing this," Adelina says with a smile.

"Yes, girl—get that man!" Havannah adds.

"Ditto, Kaia—you're amazing."

The fact that they're being so supportive means the world to me, and I start tearing up at their words of encouragement. I pause shoving things haphazardly into my suitcase and walk over to get a closer view of the screen.

"Thank you so much, you guys. Truly, I can't thank you enough…for everything."

Havannah makes a heart with her hands and holds it up to the screen, and the rest of us follow suit, laughing as we turn it into a contest to see who can hold their hands up the longest.

"Go get him, Kaia. And call us as soon as you can!" Callie says. "I don't care what time it is here, I need to know how it goes!"

Panic pangs in my chest, and I take a deep breath to calm myself.

"I will," I say, flashing them a smile, laced with just a hint of uncertainty.

The next day, I get to the airport with literal hours to spare, because that's just who I am as a person. Besides, I have enough to stress about as it is, so I'm trying to limit it wherever I can.

I check my bag and make my way through security, flicking my wrist to check the time on my watch for the fifth time in the last two minutes, and I can practically hear the girls' laughter in my head. They'd for sure be making fun of me for this bit of travel anxiety—stressing about the possibility of missing my flight, and I've been here for less than 30 minutes.

Security wasn't terrible—the line moved steadily, though I did get a stern talking-to from a TSA agent for still having some water in my Hydroflask. I chugged it before heading right for my second cup of coffee for the day.

The coffee shop is situated right off the security checkpoint and miraculously, there are only a few people in line. I'm more than ready for the comfort of my warm and yummy mocha, settling in at my gate, and finishing the book that I've been working on since Paris.

"Morning! I'll take an eight-ounce mocha, please," I say to the cheery barista, "Also, I love your hair."

Her hair is a beautiful bright pink with shimmery highlights in it. I don't know if I'd ever have the bravado, but it has me thinking about visiting the nearest hair salon as soon as I get to Paris. Isn't that what you're supposed to do when your heart is broken? Make some drastic changes to your hair?

I exhale and remind myself I'm not heartbroken.

At least not yet.

"Thanks!" she says with a smile, a piercing poking out from under her top lip. I pull out my credit card and extend it in her direction to pay for my coffee.

"Oh, the person in front of you paid for your coffee. You're all set!"

"Oh, wow! That's the best way to start this trip," I say, genuinely surprised. I don't see anyone waiting for their coffee, so they must've come and gone without me noticing.

"Well, then I'd like to pay for the next person who

comes by," I say with a smile, inspired by the random act of kindness. I purchase a gift card and the barista lets me know she'll use it for whoever comes by next. I grab my drink, then check the time and my boarding pass again as I head to find my gate.

My gate is a bit of a trek from the coffee shop, but not a problem, because I checked my big bag, leaving me with my backpack and a crossbody purse. Also, I don't have to rush. My flight doesn't leave for another two hours, and while some would think that it's utterly ridiculous to be at the airport this early, I can't think of anything better than the stress-free wait and reading my book.

After a good walk and a quick tram ride, I find my gate number and start walking over to settle into a seat to read and charge my phone. I look down to put my boarding passes into my purse as I approach, feeling a weird sort of sixth sense that must just be deja vu from my last trip to Paris. That is until I look up and am greeted by three familiar faces.

Callie, Havannah, and Adelina are sitting in a row at the gate, smiling up at me, waving me over, obviously giddy about pulling one over on me.

I'm stunned. I'm absolutely frozen where I'm

standing, and honestly wondering if maybe I'm having a stroke and hallucinating my best friends at the airport right now, at my gate, with passports in their hands.

"There's no way," I finally say, to no one in particular.

"Oh, better believe we couldn't let you go to Paris alone, Kaia!" Adelina jumps up and hugs me.

"How did you—" I manage to get out before Havannah is on her feet.

"Come on, I know you don't think you're the only one who can book a last-minute flight! We were not letting you do this alone." She wraps her arms around me.

"We've got your back, Kaia. I know how much courage this is taking, so we want to be here to support you. Plus, we want to eat more croissants, so it's a win-win." Callie jumps into the hug, and we all laugh.

As I'm laughing, I realize I'm also crying, but these tears are from the extreme joy that these girls show up for me in absolutely every facet of my life. I'm so moved by them being here—dropping what they're doing to go to Paris with me. Honestly, I can't believe it, especially after how I've acted over the course of the past few weeks.

"I don't know what to say. You guys mean the world to me."

Havannah laughs. "Well, that's good, I'm glad because…do you know how early I had to wake up to get my ass here at the same time we knew you'd be here?"

CHAPTER 29: JACK

"Yeah, I just landed," I say into my phone, stepping onto the familiar red carpet covering the floor at Charles de Gaulle airport. I look ahead to see a younger kid and his family at the gate next to mine holding up a handmade sign, covered in glitter, that reads, "*Bienvenue*! Welcome to Paris!"

"Be careful, son, and have a wonderful trip," my dad says on the other end. I can hear the exhaustion in his voice, and I feel a pang of guilt for not being there.

"Are you sure you're okay, Dad? I can be back on a flight in a day if you need me to. I don't—"

He cuts me off before I can finish. "I'm okay, Jack. Gran is okay. This trip will be good for you.

Please, go enjoy yourself, and tell Lachlan I said hi."

I take a deep breath and let it out slowly, releasing some of the tension in my shoulders along with it. "Okay, I will. Thanks again, Dad. Love you. Give Gran a kiss for me."

I hang up and send a quick text to Lachlan, letting him know I've landed, before making my way to baggage claim.

My dad surprised me with a flight to Paris last week. He said he felt bad that my trip was cut short after I came home to help him with my gran. I insisted that I stay back and help with the caregiving duties—taking my gran to her physical therapy appointments and helping with her medications, but he wouldn't take no for an answer.

Even my gran was on his side. We were all in the living room when he surprised me with the ticket. When I told him I should probably stay put, my gran chimed in with, "Don't be a dummy! Go to Paris!"

She's feisty, that one.

We spent the rest of the evening listening to Gran's stories of her travels when she was younger, including a solo trip to Paris where she apparently met and had a drink with a well-known artist. When I asked her who, she simply looked at me and winked behind a soft smile.

"She won't tell me either," my dad chimed in.

"Alright, keep your secrets, Gran," I teased, "And I guess I'll go to Paris, but only because I don't want you to think I'm a dummy."

"Atta boy," she said, reaching over to give my hand an affectionate squeeze.

I hadn't told them that the thought of Paris makes my chest go tight, thinking about the last time I was here and the heartbreak that came along with it. Or the ways in which I've done everything possible to distract myself from the thought of Kaia since that day at the gelato shop. Not that I've been successful. She's all I've thought about since, in between pockets of worrying about my gran and Dad.

But here I am, in Paris again, walking through the airport to meet Lachlan for a week-long redo of my initial trip.

My phone buzzes in my pocket, and I pull it out to see a text from Lachlan.

Lachlan: On my way, brother! This couldn't come at a better time. My week's been garbage. Can't wait to blow off some steam with my best mate.

As long as his idea of *blowing off some steam* doesn't involve hitting the bar every night until one in the morning, it sounds perfect to me.

Me: You and me both. See you soon, mate, I type in response.

I look up and see the large display board of departing flights, and my eye catches on the word Seattle.

Kaia girl.

The name flashes through my head before I can stop it, unable to ready myself for the emotional punch to the gut it causes. She's not *my* Kaia girl anymore. She's just Kaia, and she's in Seattle, probably at an incredible new job helping a lot of people, because that's who she is. She's amazing. I love her. Perhaps one day I'll be able to think about her without feeling like someone is ripping my heart out of my chest. Not today, but one day.

I shake off the thought and attempt to steel my heart, which is threatening to crack in two all over again, just as my hunter-green suitcase comes down the conveyor belt at baggage claim. I call Lachlan after hauling my bag off, and he answers on the first ring. "Hey, mate. Got my bag, where should I meet you?"

"Right outside in the pickup lane, mate. Look for the red."

Look for the red?

I head outside, scan the line of cars waiting in the pickup lane, and see Lachlan in the driver's seat of what looks to be a brand-new, ruby-red Bronco. A ragtop Bronco, that is. The top is down, leaving a clear view of his signature Lachlan smile beaming below his sunglasses.

I reach in and set my suitcase in the backseat, careful not to scuff the pristine fabric of the seats. This car literally looks like it's the first time it's ever been driven, or even sat in for that matter.

"New car?" I ask, greeting him with the seated version of the goofy handshake we've been doing for years.

"What, this old thing?" He shoots a dramatic wink in my direction, patting the side of his door a couple times. "Yeah, I picked her up this week. You like it?"

"*She's* beautiful, Lach. Hope you two are very happy together," I joke as we pull out of the airport terminal.

"Wanna go for burgers?" he asks, the excitement in his voice palpable. There are a select few things that Lachlan needs to be content, and burgers are one of them.

"Sounds great to me, mate." I lean back against the headrest, my thoughts drifting to Kaia again as I look out at the skyline. Always Kaia.

CHAPTER 30: KAIA

"Kaia!" Lachlan shouts from where he's sitting at a table outside the cafe we planned to meet at. He jumps up and goes in for a hug the moment I'm close enough to reach him.

"Hey, mate! I can't believe you're in Paris again. Welcome back!" He pulls out a chair and gestures for me to sit. "Here, sit! Tell me everything."

"Everything, huh?" I sigh, but my veins are still completely buzzing with the adrenaline from booking this flight, having the girls show up for me at the airport, and most of all, knowing I'm going to be seeing Jack again.

I order a latte, take a deep breath, and I dive into a full-on story time about everything that's happened the past few weeks, starting with my developing feelings for Jack, my self-sabotage from my fear of it not working out, and running home.

"Wow, Kaia. It's been a whirlwind, hasn't it, mate?" He takes a sip of his coffee, his watch flashing on his wrist as he raises and lowers his mug. "Look, I'm sorry about all the stuff between us…or lack thereof. I was stupid and drunk for most of it. But that doesn't make it right, and I'm sorry."

He pauses, but I can tell there's more he wants to say.

"I was an idiot at my party. I shouldn't have put you on blast like that, but I meant what I said. I could tell that you and Jack liked each other. I mean, we all saw how you looked at each other. And I *do* think you guys are on some soulmate-level stuff. I'm behind you guys one hundred percent. How can I help while you're here?"

I smile at him.

"It's okay, Lach. You've been a good friend," I say, and I mean it. He really has done a lot. And he *is* the catalyst for why Jack and I finally acknowledged our feelings for one another. "I appreciate you," I add, reaching over to grab his hand and give it a quick squeeze. "As far as help goes, I have no idea. I'm embarrassed to admit this, but for once I don't have a plan."

A smile spreads across Lachlan's face, and he immediately begins digging a hand through his briefcase. Eventually, he pulls out what looks to be a house key and slides it in my direction.

"I do," he says enthusiastically, a smile still plastered on his face, and I can't tell if I should be excited or nervous.

I look up at the beautiful walk-up apartment and smooth my hands over my jeans. Ivy climbs up the facade of the cream building and ends around the black-framed windows. As I grip the wrought iron railing of the front steps, I realize I'm already sweating, and I'm not even at the front door yet. I take a small step up to the landing and steel myself, attempting to look as if I've got control of my emotions when the reality is my heart is about to beat out of my chest. Lachlan's plan was essentially giving me the key to his place, where Jack is staying, and telling me that he'd be out for a couple of hours and would check in later. To which I responded that I'm not going to just unlock the door and walk in without giving Jack a warning. He still insisted I take the key in case I wasn't able to get in and to let me know if he needed to stay out later. That last part was coupled with several suggestive winks.

I force myself up the stairs and make a fist to knock on the door. I hesitate, notice I'm shaking, and take a deep breath, steadying myself.

I can do this.

I knock on the door before I can talk myself out of it and immediately fly back home to Seattle.

Footsteps approach the door.

Listen, there have only been a few times in my life when I thought I might throw up out of sheer nervousness, and…this is one of those times.

Wouldn't that just be wonderful?

Who wouldn't want to make out and run off into the sunset with me after that?

The lock clicks as it turns, and the door opens slowly until I'm face to face with the handsome golden-haired boy I've spent every day thinking about for the past who knows how many weeks.

"Kaia." Not a question, but a statement. He looks

truly shocked.

"Hey, Jack," I say timidly.

I have my hands behind my back, mostly because I don't know what to do with them. He stares a second longer, confusion setting in for him and panic for me.

This was a terrible idea. He probably hates me. I should turn around and leave while I still can.

"Uh, do you wanna come in?" he asks.

"Sure. Thanks." I step inside and place my bag on the bench in the foyer.

"Lachlan's out for a bit, but he should be back soon."

I rub the back of my neck. "I know. He's the reason why I'm here."

Hurt flashes across his face, and I realize my mistake a moment too late. "*Oh*. Understood," he says stiffly.

"I just mean, he told me you were back in Paris…" I stammer. "I'm here to see *you*, Jack."

He looks me in the eye, and he genuinely seems surprised by that.

"You came all the way to Paris to see *me*?" he asks, stepping closer to me.

I nod. I wonder if he knows I'd travel the whole

world and back simply to be in the same room as him.

"You know you have my phone number, right?" The ghost of a smile appears in the way one corner of his mouth raises.

If only he knew the number of times I had his contact pulled up and almost called him, texted him, sent him a meme…

"This had to be face to face."

"So you…jumped on a plane…crossed the ocean…"

"I know—it was rash, but I came to apologize," I start to say, but the tears come sooner than I expect. Much sooner, and much more intense than I'm prepared for. "Sorry, I just—"

Jack hesitates a moment, but he steps closer and reaches out to brush away a few tears. "Shh, it's okay, Kaia."

Things with Jack were always so easy. Being around him is so easy. *How did I ever walk away from this?*

His hand lingers on my cheek, and I reach up to hold it there. "I'm so sorry, Jack. I was scared and I didn't know what else to do." The tears continue. "I didn't mean to hurt you."

"I know you didn't."

I'm not sure how it's possible, but my heart breaks even more. I knew I hurt him by leaving the way I did, but to hear confirmation from him, to see the pain in his features at the memory of that night only intensified the downward spiral of guilt.

"I know what I did wasn't okay…and I hate that I hurt you. I just…I had to come back. There were no other options. I had to see you, to tell you *in person* how sorry I am. And that's all I'm here for. It's okay if you can't forgive me. It's okay if we'll never be—"

He gently cuts me off with his soft smile that I love so much, "It's okay, Kaia girl," he says, his voice soothing my jagged edges.

Kaia girl.

I close my eyes and savor the sound. "I missed hearing you call me that."

He steps even closer now. His face hovers above mine. "I missed saying it. More than you know." He leans down to whisper in my ear, and I feel it in my entire body, "My Kaia girl."

I close my eyes and breathe in the scent of him. I'm halfway across the world from the place I live, yet

I feel right at home. Right here, with Jack. Tears are still falling, but an undeniable sense of peace has come over me in Jack's presence.

He pulls back to look at me and wipes away the tears staining my cheeks.

"I understand if you're still upset with me and would rather not continue…whatever this is. But…" I look down at my hands and then back up at him. "For what it's worth, Jack, I love you."

He pauses and cups my face, eyes going glassy. "*For what it's worth*? Kaia, that's worth *everything. You* are worth everything. And I love you, too, Kaia."

I smile up at him, reach my arms around his torso, and hold on like I never plan to let go. Which I don't. Never again. He hugs me back and kisses the top of my head, his fingers tracing circles on my lower back.

"I didn't know if I'd ever see you again. Not in the way I wanted to, anyway," he says, and I feel the warmth of his breath on my neck as he speaks.

"I didn't either. I'm sorry, Jack, I—" I start to say, and he pulls back to look at me.

He cups my face with his hands, his face serious. "Hey, it's ok. You've already apologized. I forgave you the second you walked away that last night in Paris. It hurt like hell, but I understand why everything happened the way it did. And to be clear, I want this. I want you." A slow smile spread across his face as he spoke, blooming into a full grin.

He leans in and kisses me, his arm wrapping around my waist. "No more apologizing, Kaia girl."

The kiss is unhurried but intense. It's pure magic, electricity pulsing everywhere his touch meets my skin.

I pull back slightly, my lips still touching his. "I hope you know that I'm never letting you go, Jack Thompson. I'm not known for making the same mistake twice."

He smiles big as he rests his forehead against mine. "That'd better be a promise, Kaia Griffen."

I think about it, what it really means to never let go of Jack. It means more days like this, wrapped in each other's arms, hurried kisses as he hands me my coffee while I'm running out the door, late to work. It means sitting with each other through hard things, knowing we don't have to face the mess life throws our way alone. It means a *full* life. I know it does.

"I promise," I say, letting the full weight of what that means hang in the air around us.

His face as it splits into a true smile, showcasing his laugh lines and making his eyes sparkle. He leans in to kiss me once again, and it feels like a silent promise of the future he sees for us.

"My Kaia girl," he whispers against my lips, and I melt, wanting to stay like this forever.

Unfortunately, my stomach lets out a not-so-discreet grumble, which makes sense because I've only had coffee in the last twenty-four hours.

"Any chance we can redo that gelato date?" I ask, looking up at the man who holds my heart, who *is* my future.

He hugs me, and his laugh rumbles against my body. "Of course, we can. I'll take you on weekly gelato dates if that's what you want."

"Don't you dare tease me. Not when it comes to gelato," I say with a coy smile.

"Who, me? No way. I'd never get between a girl and her gelato," he says, lacing his fingers through mine.

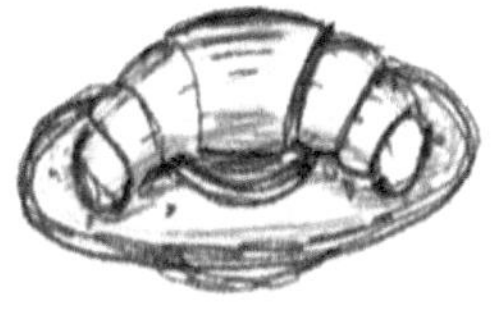

EPILOGUE

"Croissant, my love?" Jack calls from the kitchen. It's our Saturday tradition to eat croissants with our coffee, very reminiscent of our time in Paris.

"*Oui!*" I respond, but he's already walking toward me with two croissants because my answer is *always* yes.

True to my word, I hadn't let him go since that day we reunited in Paris about eleven months ago. He leans down and kisses me like he's done every morning since. I have long since stopped questioning how we got so lucky to find each other the way we did, but I don't think I'll ever fully understand what I did to deserve such an amazing man to call mine. Jack makes me feel seen and heard. He makes me feel beautiful. He makes me feel like I can do anything I set my mind to, and that I can truly make a difference in this world. It's hard to imagine my life before him, and I'm glad I never have to experience that again.

I glance down at my left hand to admire, for the millionth time, the vintage ring on my ring finger. It's a dainty gold band with a simple oval-cut diamond on top. I'll never forget flying home to tell my family and the girls. I surprised them at one of our girls' nights, which were becoming slightly less frequent since Lina got an incredible job opportunity as an art director for a company out in California, and she splits her time between San Francisco and Seattle. Callie and her new beau have settled into their routine and even adopted a new puppy together, named Lilly. Callie didn't end up with Jules from Paris, but I'll never get tired of hearing her retell the story of how she was immediately smitten with her boyfriend, Ezra, who she met on our flight *home* from Paris.

I'll never forget how we spent basically the entire evening on Havannah's living room floor while we stared at the new ring that I couldn't believe I got to call mine, reminiscing about Paris and dreaming about weddings until the sun went down.

Jack proposed about six months ago. We were in Australia—Perth to be exact, and it was my first time visiting and meeting his dad and grandma. And boy, was I nervous. Jack had to calm me down the entire car ride to their house, assuring me that I had nothing to worry about and that they were going to love me.

Ten minutes into our time spent at their house, I forgot all about how much I wanted them to love me because I was distracted by how much *I* loved *them*. They were so warm and inviting and treated me as though I'd been part of the family for years. His gran and I sat on the porch and talked about every possible thing you could imagine—dreams, zodiac signs, fast food, thrifting, Taylor Swift—she's a Swiftie, who would've thought?—and even death. You name it, we talked about it, and I left feeling sort of like I had just left a therapy session and also made a new best friend.

On our second day there, Jack wanted to stop by a "must-see" lookout spot he used to go to in high school. "It's a quick hike, but I promise you, the view is worth it," he said.

I jokingly whined about how tired I'd be after the hike, but I'd follow him anywhere.

We got to the top, and his promise rang true—they always have—the view was worth it. We had a stunning view of the Perth skyline all lit up at night. I took a step back, anticipating I'd settle into Jack for a snuggle, but nearly tripped instead, and quickly spun around.

My heartbeat intensified and tears sprang to my eyes as I saw Jack down on one knee, extending the most beautiful ring I've ever seen in my direction, the one I get to wear every day for the rest of my life.

I immediately threw my hands to my mouth out of pure shock, because I truly didn't see this coming. I mean, sure, we had talked about the future in the broad sense of the term and had some great deep conversations over a bottle of red wine about potential kids, or where we'd live after we stopped traveling, but I thought maybe I'd pick up on *something* before he popped the question. Standing there in utter shock, tears rolling down my face, I was obviously wrong. He went full stealth mode for this one.

He chuckled as if he knew what was running through my head, "I was hoping to surprise you, the way you surprised me in Paris, and so many days since then. I love you, Kaia girl. Please continue making me the happiest man alive by agreeing to be my wife and letting me love you for the rest of forever."

Crying in what I wish was a cute way, but actually had mascara running down my face, I lowered my hands and moved toward him, motioning for him to stand.

He rose, looking a little worried and I realized I hadn't said anything in response to his proposal yet.

I threw my arms around his neck and whispered, not fully trusting my voice, "I meant it when I said I was never letting you go." I kissed him. "Yes, Jack. A thousand times, yes."

Before I could pull away, Jack's arms came around my back as he twirled us both around before setting me back on my feet.

He took my left hand and slowly slid the ring on my finger, his hands much steadier than mine. "We'll get it resized," he said as he lifted my hand to his mouth and slowly kissed it.

I pulled him close and stood up on my tippy toes, and he met me halfway in an urgent kiss. One that said, *I wish we weren't in public right now.*

"I love you, Jack," I said between kisses.

"In more ways than you know, I love you, Kaia girl. I can't believe I'll get to call you my wife."

"Ay, mate—I don't see any pictures of me on that gallery wall behind you. I can send ya one if you need it!" Lachlan jokes on the other end of his FaceTime call with Jack.

Lachlan is back in Paris after a couple of weeks in Greece, and Jack and I have been spending some time in the Gold Coast of Australia until we figure out where we want to put down roots.

And if someone would've told me I'd be living like a lovestruck vagabond a couple of years ago, I would've called them crazy and proceeded to have an anxiety attack.

I feel proud of myself for loosening my grip on my desire for control over my life and really have leaned into simply experiencing it for what it is. Don't get me wrong, I still have anxiety and I still lean toward control sometimes. I'm only human. But I no longer let it dictate my life, and witnessing Jack's unfettered love of life and adventure has helped a lot. He's pretty amazing, I'm a lucky gal, blah, blah, blah

—which is what I think my friends probably hear at this point with how much I gush over Jack.

"It's just temporary decor mate. We'll be sure to include a giant poster of your face in our future home." He smiles, winking at me out of the corner of my eye.

"Saw that," Lachlan says.

"Saw what?" Jack feigns offense and throws his hand over his heart.

Taking a complete left turn in the conversation, Lachlan yells, "Hey, Kaia…is, uh, your spunky friend with the long hair going to be at the wedding?"

"Um, you're gonna have to be a lot more specific than that," I say with a laugh.

"You know, the one with the song named after her. She should have a hundred songs named after her."

"OH! Havannah? Yeah, of course. She's a bridesma—wait. Why?" I ask, moving my face closer to the screen as if that's going to make him answer quicker.

"Oh, no reason, just wondering. Okay, gotta go—bye!"

The screen goes black, leaving me and Jack staring at our reflections.

"Oookay. I wonder what that was about?" Jack looks at me with a slight smile, feigning confusion.

I've never seen that man end a conversation so quickly. Usually, I'm wondering how it's possible he can talk about nothing for as long as he does.

"Hm, it's interesting that's for sure," I say, smiling and nodding like I'm Nancy Drew on the brink of cracking the investigation wide open. The case: Lachlan might very well have feelings for Havannah.

That's right, Lachlan—I'm on to you.

Jack looks over at me with a smile. "Oh no, you're scheming, aren't ya? You got that mischievous look on your face, mate."

"I don't have any idea what you're talking about, Mr. Thompson." He pulls me onto his lap and kisses me sweetly, wrapping his arms around me. He presses his forehead into mine and smiles.

Not moving from my place on his lap, I pull out my phone and head to my Favorites, a picture of Havannah behind the bar of the Irish Pub in Paris popping up as the call begins to dial.

ACKNOWLEDGMENTS

Writing this book came slowly at first and then all at once, and I'm so thankful for those who had a hand in bringing this book to life!

To my sweet husband, thank you for your endless support and for lending your artistic talents in drawing all of the beautiful chapter header sketches.

Huge thank you to the incredibly talented Noemi De Feo, for helping me bring the cover design to life.

To my amazing friend, Amanda Lamb, thank you for helping plan an unforgettable trip to Paris all those years ago and for lending your writing genius to early edits of this story. And to Sonia and Chels for making that trip the Parisian girl's trip of my dreams.

Thank you to my fantastic editor, Amanda Chaperon. You are a joy to work with and I'm so thankful for your help in polishing my words.

To the early readers and supporters of C'est La Vie Guarantee, *merci beaucoup* - your support and feedback mean the world to me.

Dear readers, words can't express how thankful I am for you reading and supporting my work. This book was written in many in-between moments—-while my son was napping, early mornings over cups of coffee, late nights through blue light glasses, at the kitchen table, in the car. Thank you so much for taking a trip to Paris with Kaia and her pals. These characters were such a joy to bring to life, and I hope you enjoyed getting to know them.

ABOUT THE AUTHOR

Emily Cruz is a passionate writer + author, an avid coffee lover, a proud mother, and a tenth-level high-elf wizard in Dungeons & Dragons. Having fallen in love with the art of writing at a young age, she enjoys crafting funny and feel-good stories, full of relatable characters. She hopes that her writing will inspire + capture the mood of sharing a coffee with a dear friend.

You can find Emily spending her free time drinking iced mochas, making memories with her wonderful family + friends, and thinking about what color to dye her hair next.

Instagram: @emilycruzwrites

www.ingramcontent.com/pod-product-compliance
Lightning Source LLC
Chambersburg PA
CBHW020338010826
48970CB00012B/1564